TRUTH HAS
NO AGENDA

Truth Has No Agenda
Published by Blue Dragon Publishing, LLC
Williamsburg, VA
www.BlueDragonPublishing.com
Copyright 2023 Dawn Brotherton
ISBN 978-1-939696-83-0
ISBN 978-1-939696-84-7 (epub)
Library of Congress Control Number: 2022950468

TRUTH HAS NO AGENDA

DAWN BROTHERTON

 Blue Dragon Publishing

Other books by Dawn Brotherton

Jackie Austin Mysteries

The Obsession

Wind the Clock

Eastover Treasures

The Dragons of Silent Mountain

Untimely Love

Chapter 1

Lieutenant Colonel Robert Webster stood at the window, staring at the mix of Huey helicopters, fighter jets, and the bulkier C-130s on the runway. *It's happening again,* he thought. Anger and frustration warred in his gut, turning his stomach sour.

A knock at the door drew his attention.

"Sir, Senior Airman Nelson is here to see you," his executive officer said from the doorway.

"Send her in."

The executive officer nodded, and a moment later, the airman entered, precise in her uniform. Walking around to the front of his desk, he greeted her with an outstretched hand. "Good morning, Airman Nelson. Thanks for coming."

The airman returned his firm handshake without a word.

"Have a seat." He gestured toward a chair, then took one himself. His eye caught on the frame resting on his desk. From here, the photo wasn't visible, but still he saw the two second lieutenants, bright with promise and excited for their new adventure.

She tugged at the hem of her uniform jacket then sat.

Webster dipped his head, trying to get into her line of sight so she would look at him.

"I hear you had some trouble this weekend," he said. "Do you want to discuss it?"

Nelson cleared her throat and turned her head. "Not really, sir."

Webster's eyes filled with sympathy. "It helps to talk about it."

She stared at her hands, which were fidgeting in her lap. "It was stupid. Nothing important."

"Your friend thought it was important enough to get the word to me."

She chanced a furtive glance at him. "Who would that be, sir?"

"That's not the issue. But now you're here, and I can help you."

"Whoever it was shouldn't have bothered you, sir. There isn't anything I need help with."

Webster knew most women didn't want to talk about being sexually assaulted. They felt it was a stigma that would affect their work evaluations, and unfortunately, not everyone was lucky enough to have someone like him looking out for them.

"I know you may feel that way, but you don't have to be scared anymore. I'm here to help you deal with the issue," he said.

Her neck was bent as she raised only her eyes to meet his. "Sir, there really isn't anything to deal with. I was stupid and made a mistake."

"Don't blame yourself," Webster assured her. "We all make mistakes. In this case, the mistake may be more on the part of the young man, not you."

Airman Nelson shook her head. "That's what I'm saying, sir. He didn't do anything wrong. It was consensual."

"From what I hear, you were pretty hard on yourself after it happened."

She shook her head again and looked back at her hands. "I wanted it to happen. It wasn't until after that I was kicking myself. He didn't force me or anything." She took a deep breath. "I just shouldn't have . . . given in so easily."

"Maybe he shouldn't have pressured you," Webster suggested.

"He didn't. Really!"

"Since it's been brought to my attention, that makes it a formal report," he went on as if he hadn't heard her.

"Sir, I don't want to make any kind of report," Airman Nelson said.

"At this point, you don't have a choice. I already know about it. My exec will set up an appointment for you with the Victim's Counselor." Webster stood, signaling an end to their conversation. Nelson stood automatically, following military tradition.

Webster spotted the tears in Nelson's eyes as she departed. *Another powerless young lady. When will this end?*

Chapter 2

"I, Jackie Elizabeth Austin, having been appointed a lieutenant colonel in the United States Air Force, do solemnly swear that I will support and defend the Constitution of the United States, against all enemies, foreign and domestic."

She repeated the rest of the words as her boss read them from a card. When she finished the oath with, "So help me, God," the crowd applauded, and Jackie heard her sister Alison give a whoop of approval as the general shook her hand.

"Congratulations," Major General Linda Varn said quietly. "The floor is yours." She gestured for Jackie to face the audience.

Jackie took in the crowd. Her parents stood side-by-side, clapping vigorously. Alison's smile was so broad you would have thought she was the one who just got promoted. As the audience quieted down, Alison stuck her fingers in her mouth, releasing a shrill whistle, which started another round of clapping. Her husband laughed at his wife's antics as he tried to get her to calm down. Only her eight-month-pregnant belly kept Alison from jumping up and down.

"Ladies and gentlemen, please be seated," the narrator directed from the podium. "May I introduce Lieutenant Colonel Jackie Austin."

The walls echoed once again with enthusiastic applause, only quieting as Jackie's well-wishers settled back into their seats.

She took a deep breath. "Thank you all for coming. I know for most of you it was just a chance to get out of work." She paused for the polite chuckles. "For others, it was a chance to get inside the mysterious Pentagon. Now you'll all go home disappointed to realize that it really is just a bunch of offices and cubicles. We keep all our secrets at Area 51." More polite, quiet laughter.

"I appreciate you all being here, whatever your reason. I'm truly sorry for the people who aren't here." She took another deep breath and willed herself not to get emotional. She hated watching those types of ceremonies.

As she tried to settle her nerves, she thought about the words of the oath and what they meant to her. *Against all enemies.* She understood this all too well.

That I will bear true faith and allegiance to the same. Jackie knew some people said these words without thinking them through. She had dedicated her life to this nation, even when so much had been taken from her. Now she was reaffirming she wasn't done yet. She would shoulder more responsibility to represent those who couldn't stand up for themselves.

"My best friend Kris would have loved to have planned this ceremony for me. She loved any excuse for a party." She saw a few head nods in the crowd and Alison's reassuring smile. No one laughed though; most knew about Kris's cruel, untimely death

"My husband, Stan, would have hated this part. He didn't like anything too formal. But he would have suffered through it for me because it would have made me happy to have him by my side." Jackie's voice cracked on the last words as the memory of the notification team arriving at her office in service dress three years ago filled her vision.

"But I'm focusing on the future now." She gazed at her father, taking strength from his presence. His hair was slicked back as it had always been but with much less black showing now. "The Air Force has placed great trust in me with this promotion, and I don't intend to let them down. In honor of Stan, I'm going to keep this short so we can get to the party. Thank you all for coming."

The crowd stood amid more clapping and cheers, but this time, Jackie barely heard them as she made her way back to her seat. The presiding general shook her hand, and they stood in front of their chairs waiting for their cue to exit.

"Please remain standing for the playing of the Air Force Song and the departure of the official party," the narrator read. The music began, and Jackie followed the general out as the crowd sang the words that had been ingrained in her since the first day of field training between her sophomore and junior years of college. Today, she felt them more deeply, and the pride swelling in her chest carried her away with the lyrics. "Off we go, into the wild, blue yonder, flying high into the sun . . ."

Chapter 3

$\mathbf{M}$onday morning, Jackie climbed the stairs to the Sexual Assault Prevention and Response (SAPR) office on the fourth floor of the Pentagon E-ring. The outer ring of the five-sided building was where the highest ranks hung their hats because they were the only offices with a view. Jackie's office wasn't in the paneled hall that was reserved for the headquarters of the Secretary of the Air Force, but it was just outside the glass doors, within easy reach.

"Good morning, Colonel Austin," said Master Sergeant Polk, rising from his desk at the front of the main office where he managed Major General Varn's calendar and kept the rest of the staff on track.

"Good morning, Ted," Jackie replied. "Anything interesting today?"

"The general's at the chief's standup," he said, referring to the chief of staff of the Air Force, the highest military officer for the service. "She should be back shortly. She wants you to take the ten-hundred meeting."

In her bare, gray-walled cubicle, Jackie sat behind her desk and took a moment to appreciate where she was and how far she had come. Unlike some who covered their walls with unit plaques and awards, she didn't need mementos to mark her years in the military. When she first arrived at her new duty station, she considered putting up Stan's picture, but she couldn't do it. In Germany, his picture had been face down on her desk when the notification team had come to her office. She had no desire for the constant reminder of his death or what had preceded it.

She placed her common access card into the keyboard to log in. While she waited for the machine to respond, she riffled through the folders left on her desk, trying to locate notes about the meeting.

The ten o'clock meeting was with someone from the legislative liaison office, or LL, who acted as a go-between for the Air Force and members of Congress. The subject was fairly straightforward from everything she had seen so far, but there was a state representative asking questions. Jackie would have to see if LL knew why there was interest.

The most important role of the SAPR office at the Pentagon and the base-level Sexual Assault Response Coordinator (SARC) was to ensure Air Force victims received the care and support they needed to get through a traumatic experience. The service took this mission so seriously that Jackie's boss reported directly to the secretary of the Air Force.

Her job working within SAPRO was to keep statistics, work with the experts to find a way to reduce the number of assaults in the Air Force, and educate over 550,000 airmen, civilians, and reservists under Air Force jurisdiction on how to spot the signs of assault and put a stop to it.

Jackie kept the training programs up to date, adjusting them when new information came to light or trends were discovered. Periodically, she spoke at various level training sessions for commanders, providing suggestions and techniques on how to handle this very sensitive topic.

Additionally, she had to make sure the senior Air Force officials were notified of anything uncommon that might cause interest in the media or with Congress.

The SARC was the subject matter expert in these cases at the base level. They coordinated victim care and case management for sexual assault victims from initial reporting through legal disposition and resolution of issues related to the victim's health and well-being.

All sexual assault cases were sensitive and had to be handled with care. Some garnered the attention of high-ranking civilian officials and received extra scrutiny. The outcomes of those investigations weren't any different, but the paperwork and notifications took up a lot more time.

Jackie emailed the SARC at Wright-Patterson Air Force Base in Ohio to get more details for her ten o'clock meeting, and the response came back quickly.

An airman had been accused of taking advantage of a young woman. A rape kit had been collected, and the local authorities were waiting for the results. There wasn't anything to go on at this time, but OSI was investigating. The SARC had been notified, and she had reached out to the victim to arrange counseling for her.

Jackie didn't see what the congressman's concern was at this early stage. Of course, she still didn't know which side he was calling about—the victim or the accused.

She returned to the SAPR office after meeting with the legislative liaison office. Before Jackie had a chance to log into her computer, her boss stuck her head in Jackie's cubicle. "How'd it go?"

She stood to address the two-star general officer. The slight build and feminine features contrasted with Major General Varn's no-nonsense demeanor. It wasn't that her boss had no sense of humor; one just had to take the time to get close enough to her to understand it. Her boss's dubious sense of humor aside, General Varn's high energy and need to get things right made this office the perfect working environment for Jackie.

"There isn't anything for us to do right now. The accused is from the congressman's district. The staffer reached out to see what we know."

"What does LL want to do with it?" the general asked.

"The division chief has drafted a response that basically says the investigation is still ongoing and, to ensure a comprehensive result, shouldn't be rushed. If the congressman's office contacts them again, they'll let us know and set you up to make a phone call."

"Sounds like a plan." Varn stepped away, then backtracked. "I'm going TDY next week," she reminded Jackie. "You'll have to cover all the meetings and review any new cases that come in."

"Yes, ma'am. No problem." Pride swelled in Jackie's chest to think the general trusted her to represent the office when she was on temporary duty elsewhere. When she had worked for the inspector general at her last base, she commonly sat in on wing meetings to represent her boss. Working at the Pentagon was a much higher level, and Varn had only recently been tapping Jackie to fill in for her. Maybe it was the recent promotion, or perhaps just her time in the seat. Either way, Jackie loved being in the know and contributing to the discussions about important Air Force decisions.

Varn tapped the wall of the cubby and hurried off to her next appointment while Jackie sat to log into her computer.

"Ma'am?"

Jackie glanced up. An airman, with her arms crossed and head down, stood next to Master Sergeant Polk in the opening to the cubicle. The airman's face was blotchy, and she didn't look up, even when Polk introduced her.

"Senior Airman Amanda Nelson would like to talk to

someone. I thought you would be the best choice." He looked meaningfully at Jackie. "The conference room is open."

Jackie stood and came around the desk. "Of course. Thank you, Ted. I've got this." She introduced herself to the scared young lady and guided her to the small conference room next door to the office, where she shut the door behind them.

"Amanda, I'm glad you came in. What can I help you with?"

The young airman settled herself on the edge of the chair but still didn't look up.

"Can I get you something to drink?" Jackie asked.

Amanda shook her head. "I was told you could help me." Her voice was barely above a whisper.

"I'll do what I can." Jackie took the seat beside Amanda.

"My boss is saying Mac assaulted me." For the first time, Amanda met Jackie's eyes. "But he didn't! He didn't do anything wrong."

Heart breaking for this woman, Jackie reached out to her. "Are you getting hassled because you reported an incident?"

The girl's blue eyes flashed. "That's just it. I didn't report anything. I never said Mac—Sergeant Morgan—hurt me. As a matter of fact, I specifically said he didn't."

The statement knocked Jackie off balance. "Why don't you tell me what happened?"

"Sergeant Morgan and I work together. We've gotten closer recently. He's a great guy and a wonderful listener."

Jackie waited for Amanda to gather her thoughts.

"We were drinking at a party, having a good time. One thing led to another, and we ended up back in his apartment." Amanda's face turned red at the memory.

"It's okay if you started something, but if you changed your mind and said no, he still should have stopped," Jackie said gently.

"But I didn't! That's the point! Now Jason knows, and we'll never get back together." Tears streamed down her face.

Jackie handed her a box of tissues. "Who's Jason?"

"My boyfriend. Well, my ex-boyfriend. I mean, we were going through a rough patch, but I thought we were getting back together, you know? Now everybody's heard about this stupid investigation. Mac won't talk to me. Jason's acting as if he's afraid of me." She sniffed and wiped her nose. "I hear people whispering when I walk in a room."

"But if Sergeant Morgan raped you—"

"He didn't! I'm the one who wanted to have sex!" The admission rushed out, then left her appearing defeated.

The wheels spun in Jackie's head as she tried to puzzle this out. "How did the commander get involved?"

"I have no idea. Why would he care anyway?"

Jackie was surprised at Amanda's attitude. "It's the commander's job to care," she said.

Amanda snorted, then she shot Jackie an apologetic look.

"Let's back up. Who else knew about you and Sergeant Morgan?"

"Anyone who was at the party could have seen us hanging out together," she said. "I suppose someone could have seen us leave together. I was drinking and didn't pay any attention."

"Does he have a roommate?"

"Yes, but he wasn't there, and I didn't see him Saturday morning when I left."

"Would Sergeant Morgan have said anything?"

"If he did, he wouldn't be describing it as a rape." Amanda's nose scrunched as she tucked her chin.

"No, of course not." Jackie furrowed her brow. "What about when you got back to your place? Who did you talk to?"

"No one. I went home, got changed, and went to breakfast."

"Who did you sit with?"

"Suzanne was there, but she wouldn't say something like this," Amanda said.

"Did you tell her about Sergeant Morgan?"

Amanda thought about it. "I might have said I made a mistake by sleeping with Mac when I was trying to patch things up with Jason."

Jackie leaned forward, resting her elbows on her knees. "Are you sure Suzanne wouldn't tell?"

During the bus ride home, Jackie propped her head against the window. Memories of her time as a missile launch officer at the beginning of her career swirled through her mind. As one of the first women on a co-ed crew, she'd put up with her share of harassment—and then some.

She remembered vividly what it was like to not have someone to turn to about the problem without feeling judged. Her superior officers were all men who showed no sign of comprehension when she expressed that a woman might feel uncomfortable if a man suggested a game of strip poker while in the capsule.

Just when she didn't think things could get worse, she had been stalked by a serial killer. Jackie's world had been turned upside down.

Her shoulders tightened as she recoiled from the touch her memories conjured up. She inhaled deeply and exhaled slowly, focusing on relaxing her taut muscles before it brought on a headache.

She shook herself and set her shoulders. Everything happened for a reason, and in her current job, she was in a position to help victims be heard. From her desk inside the Pentagon, she supported people across the Air Force. She had to remind herself of this whenever she was feeling worn out.

After a short ride, the bus pulled up to her stop, and she filed off. As she walked to her apartment, she wondered if things would have been different for her if people had treated her as an equal and not as a woman. Her father's words floated through her mind: *what doesn't kill you makes you stronger, but it racks up quite a hospital bill.*

He was a former policeman, so Jackie was never sure if he meant it literally or figuratively. At this point, Jackie had survived two attempts on her life, so she should have super strength by now.

Chapter 4

Sweat rolled into her eyes and her blood pounded as she worked the pedals hard. There were very few places she could really open up and get some speed on her Trek bike, so she wanted to take advantage of this stretch while she could.

Jackie missed the feeling of the wind through her hair, but in this crowded city, wearing a helmet was a must. She pedaled harder and bent low over her bike. Ahead in the distance, two lone figures appeared from around the bend. Jackie swore and slowed. She rode early in the morning to avoid as many people on the path as possible, but apparently, others had the same idea.

As she approached the duo, she nodded a greeting, and the older couple called out a cheery good morning. Jackie continued at her now unhurried pace and took the time to look around. The red and orange leaves would soon appear, but for now, the days were still hot and humid. She liked the hustle and bustle of the city, although she had also enjoyed the calm, German countryside at her last assignment.

Here, there was something for everyone. She turned off the bike path, breathing in the crisp morning air and beginning her cool-down ride through the more populated parts of Washington, DC. She tried to take in the various types of beauty around her, appreciating life in the moment. She had seen, first through her best friend and then her husband, how quickly it could be taken away. She shook her head to clear away the dark thoughts trying to invade her morning ritual. This was her cleansing time.

Jackie looked at her watch and picked up her pace. She still needed to shower and change before work.

Gliding up to her apartment complex, she tossed her right leg over the back of her bike and coasted to a stop with only her left leg on the pedal. She hopped off and pushed her bike toward the building. An elderly man held the door to allow her to wheel it inside.

"Good morning, Mr. Phillips."

"Good morning, Colonel," he replied with a twinkle in his eye.

"Lieutenant Colonel." She corrected him as she always did. Within the military, all colonels and lieutenant colonels were addressed as colonel, but Jackie enjoyed the daily morning exchange with Mr. Phillips.

"You'll get there." Mr. Phillips waved as he went out for his morning walk.

Jackie stowed her bike in the rack alongside five other bikes and moved to the elevators. While she waited, she removed her helmet and shook out her long, chestnut-brown hair. Some still clung to her face in places from the sweat, but the rest fell around her shoulders in thick waves.

At thirty-six, Jackie was not quite a fitness nut, but she was determined to keep her figure trim. She had added biking to her routine when she moved to the city, not only because it was a good workout but also because it was a great source of transportation in a pinch—when it wasn't raining.

After showering and donning her uniform, Jackie caught the bus for the few miles to the Pentagon. On the way, she scrolled the news feeds on her phone.

Getting off the bus, she joined the packs of military and civilians plodding their way through the security gates. This daily routine didn't frustrate her as it did some of her colleagues. She was awed by the sheer number of people this five-sided building accommodated. It was larger than a small city and had six different zip codes.

Jackie settled into her cubicle and poured through the files that had come in from various legal councils and major commands during the night. Sadly, her office spent more time compiling the statistics that Congress and the news media were so hungry for rather than fixing the problem.

Amanda Nelson's case from Andrews Air Force Base was still bothering her. She went to Major General Varn's office.

"Ma'am, I have an idea to run by you," she said.

"What's up? Come on in."

Jackie perched on the chair in front of her boss's desk and explained her concern about Amanda.

"There might be more going on here than what Airman Nelson is revealing to you," Varn said. "I'll talk to the wing commander at Andrews. I know he takes these accusations very seriously. Let's hear what he has to say."

"Do you want me to talk to the SARC?"

"Start there. See if she has any insight."

"I'll check her stats for unit-level engagement to find out if she needs help." Jackie made herself a note.

"You'll probably need to go to Andrews and check this out personally. Get into the squadron and poke around a bit. See if there's an issue."

Jackie's stomach knotted. "The squadron, ma'am?"

"Is that a problem?"

Jackie fidgeted. "No, ma'am. But maybe someone local would be better connected."

"I don't want someone connected. I want an outsider who

doesn't have a dog in the fight. Is that going to be a problem?" she asked again.

"No, ma'am."

"I would think you'd jump at the chance to get out of DC and your cubicle for a little while."

"I just haven't been on a base since I came back from Germany," Jackie said.

Varn's look softened, but her tone left no room for argument. "Then it's about time."

Jackie nodded. "I'll look at the calendar and set something up."

When she got back to her desk, she sank into her seat, burying her head in her hands. Thoughts of Stan and the plane crash flooded her brain. Waves of guilt assaulted her as she once again blamed the exercise scenario she had written as part of her job for Stan's death.

Since returning to the States, she had successfully buried herself in paperwork at the Pentagon, not even shopping on a military base. If she went to Andrews, she wouldn't be able to avoid the smell of jet fuel and the rumble of the engines as the aircraft took off. Distancing herself from the routine life on a base had made the tightness in her chest lessen.

She shook the thoughts away and ran an internet search on the security forces squadron commander, Robert Webster. A story from a few years back popped up from the *Air Force Times*. Major Robert Webster was being lauded as the commander who came in and cleaned up a security forces squadron that had several accusations of sexual harassment. According to the article, the commander was approached in his first week of command by a woman in the squadron who felt she was being harassed but had never felt comfortable taking her complaint to the previous commander. Webster launched an investigation and three other airmen stepped forward with similar complaints. The accused were brought to trial and the two senior non-commissioned officers were found guilty of Cruelty or Maltreatment according to Article 92 of the Uniformed Code of Military Justice.

Webster had been commended for his quick response, and the rest of the article was full of quotes from women in his squadron saying how great it was to have someone looking out for their interests.

Another article listed his name as one of a handful of officers promoted ahead of his peers to lieutenant colonel. His Facebook page showed pictures from a change of command when he took over the large security forces squadron just over nine months ago at Joint Base Andrews.

Jackie ran a quick search for Webster's name in the management system used to track sexual assault and harassment cases. His name appeared over twenty times as the commander overseeing the case and making recommendations for sentencing. Although she had never looked at the data in this way before, Jackie was pretty sure that was an unusually high number.

She checked the dates on the reports; Webster had filed six in the last nine months. The only other report from that squadron was over seven years ago. A tingly sensation crept up her spine.

She pulled up the most recent closed report and read the summary provided. A twenty-three-year-old male staff sergeant was accused of taking advantage of a nineteen-year-old female airman first-class in his unit. Sad, but not uncommon. Interesting that it was labeled as "taking advantage of" rather than assault.

The next report was similar between a technical sergeant and a lower-ranking staff sergeant. In the third, the accused was a second lieutenant who allegedly promised rewards to those under his commander in exchange for sexual favors. Some of those promises had tipped over into alleged assault.

Jackie had heard of multiple reports against the same accused before, but she had never noticed so many different accused in one squadron. Even with more than four hundred people, statistically speaking, the chances were rare.

The uptick in reporting could be that people felt comfortable talking to Webster, knowing his history. Or was there something else? That idea fought for Jackie's attention. Normally she would consider the working climate to see if leadership was overlooking this behavior, but Webster was doing the opposite.

As she tried to unravel the different strings, a silver whistle fell on the desk.

She flinched, then matched the mischievous grin of the tall, slender major standing in front of her.

"What's this for?"

"Don't tell me you forgot. Tonight's our first practice, Coach Jackie."

She draped the cord around her neck. "Think this whistle will work around the office as well as it should on first graders?"

Leon plopped down in a chair. "I don't recommend trying it out in this building. Security can be a little jumpy. And I'm not guaranteeing it will work on the kids, but it will give us some illusion of power."

Jackie smiled. She actually *had* forgotten about her promise to help Leon coach the neighborhood soccer league for his first grader and her friends. "I can use any type of power I can get my hands on."

"Vicki is really excited. She wore her soccer jersey to school today."

"But tonight's only a practice."

"Try telling that to a six-year-old. Here, you might want to brush up on these." He tossed a paperback to her, which she caught easily. "Not that the rules will help much. For the most part, kids at this age just chase after the ball or stand in the field staring at the sky."

"Assuming I actually have a social life and don't have time to sit around reading kids' soccer rulebooks, why don't you summarize it for me? What do I need to know to survive the first practice?"

"Nothing in that book. I have some drills planned. If we can get them to pay attention and kick the ball without falling over, I'll consider it a successful practice." He paused. "You do know how to kick a soccer ball, right?"

"Only slightly better than a six-year-old, but I can confidently say I've never fallen over while doing it. Text me the location for the park," Jackie said. "What time do you need me there?"

"If you can get there by six, we can set up cones and hula hoops for the drills before the kids start arriving." He pushed himself out of the chair. "Remember, show no fear."

Chapter 5

Jackie got on the road early Wednesday morning, trying to beat the rush hour traffic. Even heading out of DC at six-thirty, she still found herself sitting in stop-and-go traffic on I-395, crossing the Williams Memorial Bridge. Andrews was thirty miles from the Pentagon, but the drive would take her over an hour at this rate.

The closer she got to Andrews, the tighter the knot in her stomach got. To take her mind off being back on a base, she thought of the various people she wanted to talk to. The wing commander would obviously be her first stop, as protocol dictated. She would then touch base with the local SARC office and see if they had any thoughts about what was happening in Amanda's case.

She finally pulled into the Joint Base Andrews 316th Wing parking lot a few minutes before eight a.m., just in time for her first meeting. She grabbed her notebook and hustled up to the building.

"Colonel Austin?" an older lady greeted her when she pushed through the door to the front office.

Jackie smiled and nodded.

"Have a seat. Colonel Dellinger just called, and he's stuck in traffic. He apologized and said he'd be here as soon as possible. Can I get you a coffee?"

"No, thank you," Jackie replied, taking a seat on the long, leather sofa. She rifled through her bag, pulling out her notebook with her list of questions. She was reviewing them when she heard her name again.

"Jackie? Sorry I'm late." Colonel Dellinger offered her his hand as she rose.

"No problem, sir. Thanks for seeing me."

"You're doing me a great courtesy looking into this. Come on into my office." His southern drawl was like warm honey, making everything he said sound comforting and pleasant.

As he led her past his secretary, Jackie couldn't help but notice his tall, lanky frame. His Air Battle Uniform, or ABUs, hung on him as if he couldn't get a size long enough for his stature that didn't dwarf his 180-pound physique. Even with the typically baggy style of the ABUs, his broad shoulders captured her attention.

As he took a seat behind the large, oak desk, Jackie observed the array of artwork on the walls. It wasn't the usual military trappings that accumulate over a career. Instead, she was pleasantly surprised to see actual art. Granted, airplanes were represented, but framed prints of mountains and lakes added peaceful color and tranquility and far outnumbered the gray machines.

For a moment, she almost forgot she was on a base. When he turned to look at her, she noticed that his close-cropped hair showed a little silver, and his eyes were a brilliant clear green.

"General Varn tells me you have a concern," Dellinger said once they were both seated.

"Yes, sir. One of the airmen in the security forces squadron came to see me. She's concerned about a sexual assault charge that's been filed."

"That's Lieutenant Colonel Webster's squadron," he confirmed. "Until the recommendations come to me, I don't review any of the details. I don't want to have any influence, or appearance of influence, into any of the fact-finding. I have to make the final proposals to the generals above me."

"Understandable, sir. That's why I thought I would come down here and ask a few questions myself."

"What are you hoping to find?"

"It may be a simple misunderstanding, and the young lady just needs a voice on her side."

"Isn't that what the SARC is for?"

"That's just it. The airman didn't go to the SARC. She didn't file the complaint."

From the tilt of his head and the squint of his eyes, the confusion was obvious.

"Exactly, sir. She claims nothing happened. Well, nothing she didn't intend to happen." Jackie hoped her face wasn't as red as it felt. She didn't normally get embarrassed so easily, certainly not talking about someone else's sex life.

"Couldn't it just be that Lieutenant Colonel Webster is looking out for his subordinates? Perhaps he sees something this airman is missing?"

"Yes, sir, it absolutely could be just that. I hope it's that simple."

Dellinger's eyebrows rose. "I hear misgiving in your voice. What aren't you saying?"

Jackie took a deep breath. "When I looked back in the files, Colonel Webster was the commander or investigating officer in over twenty cases. That's higher than any other individual in our database. What's weirder is that many were never prosecuted."

"We both know that sometimes it comes down to he-said, she-said. No proof doesn't always mean nothing happened."

"I agree, sir. But even if they can't make a case for sexual assault, often they can bring a case for a lesser charge. Then, if a pattern is established, the behavior can still be stopped," Jackie said.

He squinted at her. "What's your point?"

She cringed because she wasn't doing a good job explaining her concern. "Colonel Webster had a number of his recommendations overturned at higher levels. That tells me they didn't see even enough evidence to warrant further action." She rushed on as he started to shake his head. "Most people don't see those statistics because they can't get past the higher number of accusations made to find out how many cases actually had enough proof to substantiate."

"You're saying he's accusing without gathering the evidence?" Dellinger opened a folder on his desk. "I pulled his performance reports after I talked to General Varn. Looks like Webster was brought in to fix a very troubled squadron at his last duty station. He received high marks from his rater and senior rater."

"Sir, I'm not questioning his performance or his integrity. I would just like to understand how he picks up on things that others don't. Or, if victims are more comfortable talking to him, why? Is it something we can teach others? What can we learn from him to improve the overall SAPR program?"

Colonel Dellinger leaned back in his chair, crossing his hands in his lap. Jackie's eyes instinctively followed the movement, noting the absence of a wedding band. The quickening of her heart stunned her, and then guilt reined it in to a painful slowness. Breathing deeply, she allowed her logical mind to kick in, chastising her heart for feeling as if she were betraying Stan. She was no longer married and was allowed to be interested. As the war raged on in her head, she steered her attention back to the issue.

The commander smiled at her. "The Pentagon sure has taught you how to be politically correct, hasn't it?"

"Sir?"

"You say you want to learn from him, but what actually caught your attention was that something was off. Isn't that right?" Colonel Dellinger asked. "That sounds to me as if you suspect a problem, not a solution."

Jackie blushed at being caught in her double speak. "Sir, I just meant—"

He cut her off with a short laugh. "No need to explain it to me. I did my time at the Pentagon. I understand what it means to speak carefully around higher-ranking officers all the time. You don't want to be the bearer of bad news, only solutions. Well, if this digging gets you closer one way or the other, I'll help you out."

"I appreciate that, sir. Thank you. Though I do hope I'm wrong."

"Part of me hopes you're right. The alternative is there are a disproportionate number of women being harassed in this wing, and that would be much worse."

She nodded, grateful that he understood her concern. "I have an appointment with OSI later today and will try to schedule time with the inspector general, but I'd also like to talk to the JAGs, sir."

"Prosecuting or defending?"

"Maybe both."

"For any closed cases, that won't be a problem. For anything open, I'll have to check with the senior counsel to see if there's an issue with that."

"That would be great, thank you," Jackie said. "In the meantime, I'll visit the SARC and get their read on it. I want them to know I'm on base and poking around so they don't think I'm trying to go around them."

"Like me, they'll welcome the help. It's only two people corralling a lot of volunteers. Do you know where their offices are?" Dellinger and Jackie rose from their seats.

"I've chatted with the SARC over the phone, but we haven't had the chance to meet in person."

Jackie followed him to the outer office, where Colonel Dellinger handed her off to his executive officer, telling Jackie that he'd be able to give her directions to wherever she needed to go.

"Thank you again, sir," Jackie said, offering her hand.

"Let me know if you need anything else," Dellinger replied.

The warmth of his hand in hers surprised Jackie. Her dad always told her you can tell a lot about a person from their handshake, and this handshake was telling her great things about Colonel Dellinger. She smiled at the wing commander, catching a sparkle in his eyes that she could've sworn hadn't been there at the start of their meeting.

Chapter 6

Master Sergeant Sarah Williams, the SARC on duty, greeted Jackie with a broad smile and was eager to provide the background behind the open reports. She also had a lot of helpful information about the overall climate on base.

Joint Base Andrews supported many active, air guard, and reserve units in the National Capital Region. The airlift wing on base provided airlift and communications for the president and other senior cabinet and military leaders, so the troops were typically crème of the crop.

"I've been here three years, and I've hardly ever received reports—until recently." Master Sergeant Williams looked downcast. "I'm not sure what else I can do."

"Is all your training up to date? Are the squadrons complying?" Jackie asked.

"Yes. But I haven't seen an uptick this sharp since we started the program."

Initially, when the Air Force launched its campaign to ensure all airmen knew their rights about reporting sexual harassment and sexual assault, many people had come forward, but that had leveled off after a couple of years. The increase in the number of restricted reports had shown that individuals were more comfortable reaching out for help after the start of the campaign. That was the most important thing. Those always had the potential to turn into unrestricted reports when the victim was ready to confront their attacker.

"I still have the usual number of people coming in for help or to ask questions, but I'm shocked by the number of reports made by other people on behalf of a victim," Master Sergeant Williams said. "I've been the SARC at two other bases and often the victim will be escorted in by a friend to make the report, but here, I've been receiving more reports made for someone they think has been assaulted." She tucked her hair behind her ear.

"Don't get me wrong. I'm glad people are noticing and care enough to do something about it. I'm more concerned about what we're doing wrong that the victim doesn't feel like they can report the issue themselves," Williams said.

Jackie took this in. "Have you talked to any other SARCs? Are they seeing the same thing?"

"I've called a few people I know. They hardly see any third-party reporting. If they do, it's for someone the person reporting saw at a bar or something—situations where they didn't know the victim."

"Is that's what's happening here?" Jackie asked.

"No, ma'am." Master Sergeant Williams dropped her voice, although no one else was in the office. "Most of them are coming from the security forces squadron."

Jackie gave a small smile. "It's not a secret. I've seen the statistics. That's one of the reasons I'm here."

Williams let out the breath she was holding. "What a relief. I've got friends in that squadron, and I've been trying to gather information without coming right out and asking."

"Why? Do you suspect something's off?"

Williams gave a noncommittal shake of her head. "I don't know what to think. I don't have anything concrete."

"And what do your friends think?"

"The only thing they've said is they're surprised at the people who have gotten in trouble in their squadron. A few have tried to ply me for info, but I didn't bite."

"What do you mean, they were surprised?"

"Some of the accused have been really nice guys." Williams waved a dismissive hand. "Except the lieutenant. Apparently, he was a little creepy. But the others were just doing their job and living their life. To be honest, a few guys are talking about putting in for a transfer. They don't want to be the next one accused. And the women are getting the cold shoulder. No one wants to talk to them and chance being accused of something they didn't do."

Jackie took grim satisfaction that she wasn't the only one noticing something was off. But the question was why.

"I was caught off guard by your request for a meeting," OSI Agent Thompson said after Jackie had taken her seat. He didn't even bother to stand. "I've never talked to anyone from your office before."

Jackie wondered what rank this agent was, that he didn't even show common military courtesies. She disliked the practice of OSI agents wearing civilian clothes and not using their rank, primarily because they came across as cocky. When the uniformed person didn't know the rank of their interrogator, it leveled the playing field, especially when they had to question people who were more senior to them.

But that was the point.

"I'm kind of surprised myself," she replied. "I've talked to the OSI a little *too* often." Her last contact with OSI hadn't been very pleasant—mostly because they had been trying to pin Stan's death on her.

"What can I help you with? You mentioned the security forces squadron."

"I noticed a spike in sexual assault reports from that unit. I wanted to get your take on it to see if this was usual or something to be concerned about." She had her own suspicions but needed something definitive to show her boss. She couldn't accept that a problem in a unit developed so quickly, especially when the prevention program had so much attention at all levels of the military.

"I pulled the cases after you set up the meeting." He tapped the stack of folders on his desk. "I'm glad you reached out. The reporting from that squadron is a little irregular. Not so much the number—spikes happen from time to time. I'm more concerned with how thin the files are."

"What do you mean?" Jackie pulled out a notepad and pen.

"We investigate any suspicion of sexual assault, but the cases from the security forces have little to go on. Not even victim statements."

"Does a victim have to make a statement?"

"Typically, the victim is the main witness, but nothing says they must testify. If they choose not to give a statement, we still investigate, but there isn't much to go on unless other people were present."

Jackie scratched something in her notebook. "Does it often happen that the victim doesn't make a statement?"

"There are times when it's too traumatic, and they don't want to face their attacker, but the Victim's Counsel is a lawyer available to help them through the investigation and prosecution process. But in the security forces squadron, that's not the case." He fanned out four file folders in front of him.

"In all of these cases, the victim stated no sexual assault took place."

"What? How does that even make sense?"

He tossed his hands in the air. "The identified victims don't want to press charges."

"Does that close the case then?"

"Not exactly. We still have to make sure the alleged victim isn't being pressured to recant or that there isn't some other inappropriate conduct going on."

"And if there isn't?"

He stacked the folders again. "We turn everything over to the JAG and let them make a recommendation to the commander."

"Did you find any connection between the cases?"

"No, and that's the other thing. If we were investigating the same person multiple times, it would raise red flags. All these accused were different people and various ranks. Nothing really ties them together, except for the fact that they're in the same squadron."

"Who do you interview in these cases?"

"The alleged victim, of course. Peers, best friends, the first sergeant."

"But not the commander?"

"No. The commander has final say in the process for nonjudicial punishment, so we leave them out."

"How many cases have you investigated in the security forces squadron in the past two years?" Jackie wanted to confirm the numbers she had pulled from her database.

He looked at his notes. "None until about six months ago. We've investigated four since then. Three are closed. We still have one we're finishing the paperwork on."

"Which case is that?"

He checked his notes. "Nelson."

"I don't want to get in the middle of anything you have ongoing," Jackie said. "But can I see your investigation on the closed files?" She handed him a letter from Major General Varn, authorizing Jackie access to details not released to many people.

He read over the document, noting the two-star's signature and duty title. "I'll help you in any way I can. I hate these types of investigations." He slipped the paper into his desk drawer. "But I'm going to hold on to this to cover my ass."

Chapter 7

It was a short walk to the next building where the lawyers for the victims had their offices. Even in the Air Force, the lawyers' offices seemed nicer than the general population—certainly better than her cubicle. Real honey-birch paneling covered the walls, and the seats in the waiting room were cushioned in blue upholstery.

"I admit I'm lacking in knowledge about the process at your level," Jackie told the Victim's Counselor, who led her into his office.

"I'll answer any questions I can for you. Where do you want to start?" Captain Corbin asked. He gestured for her to sit, then he sat in a chair next to her, not behind his desk. Jackie liked this captain immediately. His thoughtful consideration was suited to this job.

"What happens if the victim refuses to make a statement?"

"Depends. Is it because they are afraid or is there some other reason?"

"I'm not sure. What if someone else files the concern with the commander, but the alleged victim says nothing happened or at least won't say what happened?"

"Is this about the security forces squadron?"

Jackie was astounded. "How did you know?"

"They've been keeping us plenty busy lately. Some of the alleged victims have asked us how to get the cases dropped."

"Can you do that?"

"In a sense. We can keep them from going to trial, but we can't make the case disappear entirely. The commander has the final say."

"So even if the victim doesn't want to press charges or whatever, the commander can still punish the accused?"

"It goes toward doing what's best for the Air Force. A victim may not want to confront their attacker, but that doesn't mean we can let them go on attacking."

As that thought sank in, Jackie came up with her next question. "So it's taken out of the victim's hands?"

"There's a difference between harassment and assault, and they are treated differently. OSI investigates assault cases, but the IG looks into harassment."

Jackie nodded. She already knew that part, having worked in the inspector general's office at her last assignment.

"Either way, the findings go to the JAG, who makes a recommendation to the commander. If there's enough evidence, even without the victim's testimony, the commander can take action. There's a large range of punishments if the member is guilty."

"Don't they get kicked out?"

"That's an option, but not always. It depends on how much evidence there is. Ultimately, it's up to the commander."

To Jackie, the thought of so much power wielded by one person was upsetting, especially when most of the Air Force commanders were men—the majority of which, she assumed, couldn't begin to put themselves in the victims' shoes.

Her head was spinning as Jackie walked out of the Victim's Counselor office an hour later. Digesting the information she had been given, she realized the more questions she asked, the more she had. What he had provided would be invaluable.

Jackie realized she needed a victim's counselor to be part of the briefing team for the commanders' training curriculum.

Distracted, she reviewed the printouts collected throughout the day as she backtracked her way out of the building. She came around a corner and ran directly into a solid figure clad in camouflage. The papers in her hands spilled across the hall.

"I'm so sorry," Jackie said reflexively, stooping to pick up the information she had gathered over the past few hours.

"My fault," the uniformed man said, bending to grab some of the loose paper.

Together they gathered the documents, and Jackie shoved them awkwardly back into the folder.

As they stood, Jackie took in the soft features of the man in front of her. His full lips and short-clipped, black curls seemed out of place in the battle dress uniform pulled tight across his middle.

"Thank you," Jackie said as he handed her a stray piece of paper. She glanced at his collar, looking for his rank to determine whether or not a "sir" was required in her response.

"No problem," the lieutenant colonel said. "I hope we got everything."

She smiled politely, trying to figure a way out of the awkward situation. "Have a nice day," she said, extricating herself.

"Are you okay?" he asked. "You seem bothered."

"No, just thinking about something else," she assured him, heading toward the door.

"Are you sure?"

"Positive. Thank you."

When she reached the outer door, something clicked in Jackie's brain. In her mind's eye, she searched the lieutenant colonel's uniform again, finding the nametag—Webster!

Jackie stopped by her car to deposit what she had collected so far. Checking her watch, she decided she had time for one more office visit. Grabbing her notebook, she walked to the building adjacent to the wing headquarters.

"Not sure what I can give you that isn't already in the files." The harried major in the inspector general's office shuffled through items on his desk, finally locating his reading glasses under a pile of papers. He slipped them on and picked up his notebook. "In both cases, we determined no sexual harassment had taken place. One was clearly more an act of hazing than sexual harassment. That also isn't allowed in the military, but it's dealt with differently. I do believe the commander gave him a letter of admonishment and extra duty."

He flipped the page. "The other one wasn't as cut and dry. Definitely some flirting going on between a flight commander and one of his subordinates, but it was a two-way street. Our interviews show she flirted as much as he did, and it seemed to be mutual. The bystanders claim the comments weren't sexual in nature."

"Do you know what happened in that case?" Jackie asked.

"I think the flight commander got a letter of reprimand for fraternization and moved to a different base shortly thereafter. You'd have to ask the commander to be sure."

"Do you get many complaints of sexual harassment to investigate?"

"It's a very small part of what we investigate. It's tough to prove, so many people don't bother reporting it. It usually comes to us as part of another complaint or a climate survey."

Climate surveys were often completed when a unit got a new commander or if the headquarters suspected a problem.

"Makes sense." Jackie jotted down a note to pull the last climate assessment done for the security forces squadron.

She thanked the major for his help, and his attention was back on the computer screen before she walked out of his office.

In her car, she sorted through the information she had collected and started to read.

The paralegal in the judge advocate's office had provided her with case summaries for all the closed cases related to Webster that he had pulled from the case management system. He had also been floored by the large number—most from Webster's last duty assignment.

Six in nine months, Jackie thought. *What are the odds?*

Of the closed cases throughout his career, Webster had recommended some type of punishment in every one of the twenty-two cases. Higher headquarters had agreed with his most severe recommendation only three times: once when he was stationed at Kunsan Air Base in the Republic of Korea as a captain, and then two more at his last assignment.

More typically, a lower action such as a letter of reprimand was taken. This punishment drove an unsatisfactory annual report which inhibited promotion potential, therefore many of these airmen probably elected to separate on their own. In some situations, cases were dismissed altogether.

What is Webster up to?

Chapter 8

"Ma'am, you were looking for me?"

Jackie turned from her computer.

"Thanks for coming, Ed. I have an unusual request for you. I need some numbers run, but they are a little outside what we normally search for."

"Sure. What do you need?" Staff Sergeant Renko asked.

She handed him a slip of paper. "I'd like you to do a little research on the units Lieutenant Colonel Webster has commanded and make a comparison across the Air Force to other units of similar size."

"What are you looking for?"

"I'm not sure. You'll need to break it out by gender, perhaps by rank would be useful as well. When you find other units the same size, see how many reports of sexual harassment or assault were reported in each unit."

"You think there's something suspicious about the commander?" he asked.

Jackie shook her head. "I don't know. I'm hoping the data will show me if the number of cases reported is out of the ordinary."

"Got it. Will tomorrow be soon enough?"

She laughed at his efficiency. "More than enough. I have plenty to keep me busy."

He left her to dredge through her emails. She needed to be up to speed on anything that may come up next week when she was filling in for the boss.

She opened an email from another lieutenant colonel in the Legislative Liaison Office. The official response LL had sent Congressman Olan about the case at Wright-Patterson hadn't worked, and apparently the call from Major General Varn hadn't convinced him either. This was going to go higher. They wanted Jackie to meet with the congressman's staffer on the Hill.

The email said they would send someone from the liaison office with her to ensure she didn't make any missteps. *Great. Now they don't even trust me to do my job. If LL is so worried, why don't they handle it themselves? I have better things to do.*

She had just finished shooting an email off to her boss when the phone rang. "Lieutenant Colonel Austin," she said.

"Lieutenant colonel now? Congratulations!"

"Chaplain Vandesteeg?" She hadn't spoken to the chaplain since she began working at the Pentagon. Before that, they had been in touch weekly as Jackie dealt with the loss of her husband. "I thought you were retiring?"

"Soon, very soon. I heard you were working in the SAPR office. You're the perfect person to handle the case I'm consulting on here."

"Are you still at McGuire?" Chaplain Vandesteeg had been instrumental to Jackie discovering the truth behind her stalker, so anything he needed, she would be delighted to assist. Joint Base McGuire-Dix-Lakehurst was only a few hours' drive northeast of the Pentagon in New Jersey.

"I am. They're letting me stay in place until retirement. Probably right after the first of the year."

"Why are you involved in a SAPR case?"

"The young sergeant came to me looking for support," he said.

Jackie pulled out a pen and notebook. "Did she report the harassment to her commander, or at least go to the hospital?"

"Yes, *he* did."

"Oh." Jackie was rarely speechless, but she had never dealt with a male sexual harassment victim before. Her mind kicked into gear again. "Okay, he reported. What unit and who's the commander?"

She took notes as the chaplain gave her more information.

"He didn't go to the hospital, because in his mind, the assault was minor. I mean, she tried to get physical with him, but it wasn't anything he couldn't fend off. The real problem is the constant harassment."

"What do you mean?"

"She just won't give up. He's trying to avoid her, but it's starting to affect his work."

As he finished with the basics, he added, "Now Sergeant Davies is getting some heat for reporting."

"What? That's messed up. Who's bothering him?"

"He's feeling it from all sides. The other men in the unit are teasing him about deflecting the advances of a woman. The women are angry, accusing him of making it all up to undermine the reporting process."

"Is he?"

She felt the disapproval across the miles. "Would you be asking that question if the person making the report was a woman?" he asked.

"Yes. In one form or another. Is it a credible charge? Do you think he's telling the truth?"

He sighed. "Yes. Sadly, I think he's telling the truth, and it disgusts me that we need an office such as yours for the military."

"As a chaplain, you know better than anyone that the military is a sampling of the world."

"That is also a sad truth."

Jackie did a search through the online case management system for the case tagged with a victim named Davies. "I'm not seeing anything."

She searched by the unit and also came up blank. "Are you sure that's the right unit?"

The chaplain muttered something under his breath she couldn't make out. "Let me call the unit commander and find out why he's dragging his feet on this."

"Does Sergeant Davies know you are talking to me about his case?"

"Yes. I told him I have friends in high places. This time, I was talking about you."

Jackie chuckled. "How's he holding up?"

"He's starting to doubt himself. With so much pressure from his peers and superiors, I'm afraid he's rewriting the events in his mind. He might talk himself out of following through."

"It's unusual to have a male victim, but why all the pressure from the higher-ups? Who's the accused?"

"That's the rub. She's a civilian deputy group commander who has hobnobbed with some pretty influential people, both here and in DC." The drum of his fingers on the desk echoed through the phone line.

"Is she in his chain of command?"

"Yep. And she hand-selected him for a TDY she was going on. When he requested permission from his immediate supervisor not to go, everything came out. He had to explain how she made him uncomfortable with her comments and inappropriate touches."

Jackie shivered. It brought her back to her time as a lieutenant when she was on crew duty. As one of only a handful of women in the missile career field, the unwanted attention should have come with hazardous duty pay. Back then, there was no office like the one she worked for now. Many women had suffered in silence.

"I'll give my boss a heads-up. I have a feeling this is going to get more attention than usual. Let me know what you find out from the unit," she said.

"Will do. I'm glad you're working this one, Jackie."

As she hung up the phone, she thought about the attention a male victim would draw.

Chapter 9

It was the second practice of the season, and Jackie was settling into her role as assistant coach. She tied shoelaces, wiped runny noses, and shouted encouragements as children chased after the soccer ball.

"I don't know what I'd do without you." Leon took a long swig from his water bottle.

Jackie watched the kids break into a game of tag; all thoughts of the ball forgotten. "This is so much fun. I'm glad you asked me."

"You needed to get out of the office. This gives you a good excuse to leave at a decent hour." Leon tossed his water bottle into his equipment bag. "And I noticed you're smiling a lot more lately. Is that the fresh air or have you met someone I haven't heard about yet?"

Her mind immediately jumped to Colonel Dellinger, and he took her pause as confirmation.

"Oh, so there is someone!" He wiggled his eyebrows. "Come on, tell me everything."

She shook her head. "You don't have to know everything about my life."

"But I do. With Sarah out of town, I need to hear about romance from someone. Come on, let me live vicariously through you."

"Hey, Jackie!"

Jackie sighed in relief at the excuse to be done with the conversation. Turning, she spotted Clarisse and Ellen, two of the parents she'd met at the first practice. She waved as they climbed the bleachers to watch the chaos disguised as practice. The women sipped from Starbucks cups.

A pang of jealousy hit her; she didn't even know why. Sighing, she promised herself a trip to her favorite coffee shop after practice.

"Time to get back into the fray." Leon jogged onto the field.

Picking up the hula hoops, Jackie distributed them on the grass in the pattern Leon had sketched for the next drill.

How absurd would it be to meet a guy while researching the details of a sexual assault claim? Jackie's imagination jumped in time to telling others how she had first met the Andrew's wing commander. "I was in his office telling him he didn't know how to handle his squadron commanders." *Yeah, that would be a great story.*

But when she tried to distract herself from thoughts of Dellinger, the sparkle of his eyes filled her vision, and a warmth coursed through her as hope ignited somewhere down deep. Hope that she may be able to start over.

Since Stan's death, no one had even remotely captured her attention, so the unexpected electricity at the end of their meeting had caught her off guard. Now she didn't know how to process her feelings.

Part of her was still raw and not ready to open herself up again. But she also had to acknowledge the small voice she had been pushing down, which screamed to be heard. The voice complaining about loneliness.

A tug on Jackie's shirt brought her attention to a young girl with dark, curly hair and a round face.

When Jackie knelt, the girl pointed to her scraped knee, watching for the adult's reaction to determine what her response should be.

"Why, that's a pretty color, isn't it?" Jackie asked.

The youngster looked at her knee again, considering.

"I wonder if it changes colors if we put water on it." Jackie kept up the conversational tone as she cleaned and dressed the girl's scrape with a dinosaur Band Aid.

When finished, the girl smiled at Jackie. Holding hands, they ran out to join the others.

Chapter 10

Friday morning, Jackie found herself back at Joint Base Andrews. She had arranged with the wing commander to use an office in the headquarters building to conduct interviews. It was better to get people away from the prying eyes in their workplace.

Being back on base wasn't as hard as she thought it would be. Initially the sound of aircraft engines made her jumpy, but she was getting used to it, and now the sound didn't even register most of the time. Actually, there was something to be said for walking outdoors to go to lunch or to a meeting. That was rare while working at the Pentagon. She was also thankful for an office with a real door rather than a cubicle.

Settling in at her temporary desk, Jackie reviewed the closed assault cases. Two had been forwarded to the wing commander with recommendations for non-judicial punishment, but the defense attorney from the JAG's office had been able to get the charges dropped for lack of evidence.

The third case didn't even have enough for trial, but still the accused had offered to separate under "Other Than Honorable" conditions rather than go under the microscope and chance getting a "Dishonorable Discharge." Jackie wasn't sure what else he was doing that he didn't want to come out, because the assault case was very weak.

She was starting her day with Lieutenant Colonel Webster's first sergeant. The "shirt" was a commander's right-hand person and was closest to the heart of the unit.

"Thank you for coming in, Sergeant Preston."

Preston cut a striking figure in his camouflage uniform. With sleeves rolled up just above his elbows, the mermaid tail tattoo on his left forearm caught Jackie's eye. His broad shoulders left no extra room in the uniform shirt that looked baggy on many men.

"Anything I can do to help. Is there something specific you needed to discuss?"

"Part of my job at the Pentagon is to spot trends in case we need to adjust our training. I noticed a spike in SAPR cases coming from your squadron."

Preston crossed his legs but said nothing.

"You've been with Colonel Webster for how long now?"

"I got here shortly after he took command."

"Is Colonel Webster well liked?"

"Absolutely. He's a hard worker and cares about his troops."

Jackie gave him a conspiratorial smile. "Do you think he's *too* likeable?"

"What does that even mean?"

"Does Colonel Webster's leadership foster the kind of laid-back behavior that could roll over into harassment? You know, letting inappropriate jokes slide. Making comments he shouldn't just to be one of the guys."

"Ma'am, with all due respect, Colonel Webster is a great commander. Everyone loves him. But he keeps a professional distance. He does not fraternize with the troops."

"Why do you think there are so many cases of sexual assault and harassment in your unit?"

"I don't think there are any more in our unit than anywhere else in the Air Force. People are just more willing to come forward. They know they'll be heard."

Jackie mulled that over. It was in line with why he was brought in to clean up the problems at his last unit.

"What are you doing to address these cases?"

"The victims are getting the help they need." Preston tipped back in his chair, lifting the front legs slightly off the ground. His muscles flexed as he crossed his arms in front of his body.

Jackie wanted to wipe the smug look off his face.

"But what are you doing to change the overall climate of the unit? There has to be a reason for the spikes."

"We are cleaning out the people who are preying on younger troops."

Jackie waited for more, but nothing was offered. "Have you increased training?"

"Things will right themselves. Colonel Webster just needs time to work his magic. He'll have the squadron on track in no time."

The platitudes did nothing to boost Jackie's confidence. Biting back a retort that would be totally unprofessional, Jackie settled for, "Let's hope he's on the right track."

As Jackie walked the shirt to the door, she caught sight of Dellinger heading her way. Self-consciously, she smoothed back her hair. His crooked smile gleamed across the distance, and her heart responded.

Is he coming to see me? Should I go back inside? What if he isn't coming to see me and I'm just standing here like a dope?

She didn't have time to decide her next move before he was in front of her.

"How's it going?" he drawled. "Do you have everything you need?"

I wish.

Jackie tried to match his smile. "Everything's fine. Thank you, sir. Still working my way through a list of questions."

"Must be nice to get away from the Pentagon for a while. I

was stationed there as a major. Could never quite figure out the numbering system of those half-hallways."

She laughed. The offices were conveniently identified by the floor number, the ring letter, the spoke, then the room number. But he was right. The half-hallways, which landed in between the spokes, had a numbering system she couldn't follow.

"I've set a personal goal of walking all seventeen and a half miles of hallway in that building before I leave."

"Don't forget to drop breadcrumbs. The two floors underground always gave me the creeps." He mock-shuddered.

His phone buzzed and he held it up to read the screen. "I'm off to my two o'clock meeting. It's good to see you."

Without waiting for an answer, he continued down the hall. Good thing, because Jackie couldn't think of a proper response. She watched him go, wishing she had said something clever.

Her next interview was with one of the witnesses for the accused, who had been cleared of any wrongdoing. He crossed the room and threw himself into the waiting chair. He didn't waste any time coming right to the point.

"If I may speak openly, ma'am, this witch hunt is bullshit."

Jackie was unnerved by the venom in the major's tone.

"What makes you think this is a witch hunt?"

"People are oversensitive. Because the media has said there's a sexual assault problem in the military, now everyone sees it in every glance or comment. Why can't people just be respectful? Hell, how are people supposed to date anymore? You can't ask someone out without being accused of harassing them. That is, unless you're good looking. Then it's okay; the standards are crap."

Jackie nodded in understanding. She had heard similar

arguments at every level, and she appreciated the straight-forward way this major spoke.

"Would you feel the same way if it was your sister being harassed?" Jackie tried to reason.

"Yes, ma'am!"

She was stumped for her next line. That question usually gave people a pause, but obviously the major wasn't going to back down from his position easily.

Before she could continue her line of questioning, he added, "It's because of over reporting that the real problems are getting buried.

"If male commanders are afraid of accusations every time they try to chastise their troops, how can we ever achieve good order and discipline? Some chick is late to work and gets written up; all she has to do is claim the commander is picking on her because she's a woman. She doesn't even have to prove he's doing anything wrong. He has to prove he *didn't*. How do you prove a negative in this case? Every situation should be case-by-case. That's the best way to lead people—not as a cookie cutter."

When he stopped to take a breath from his rant, Jackie jumped in. "This is clearly a sore point with you."

"Don't get me wrong. I know there are some guys who take advantage of a situation. But I also think there are some women who take advantage. Women get accused of sleeping their way to the top. I know that's crap for the majority of women, just like I know some women who have used their sexuality—and bragged about it." He sat back in his chair, throwing out his arms in a helpless gesture.

"So why is it so hard to believe that there are some women who are true victims, and others who are only playing the part of the victim when things don't go their way? I find it harder to believe, all of a sudden, women are being attacked every time we turn around." He finally seemed to run out of steam.

"Some say it's because they feel more empowered to talk about it now. They were afraid to come forward before because no one would believe them," Jackie said.

"Is that what you believe?"

She paused thoughtfully. "I do believe some women were afraid to come forward."

"Do you think some of them kept their mouth closed because the sex card was working for them?"

"What do you mean?"

"I mean flirting, light touching, and innuendos got them noticed. As long as it also got them an extra chance or two to be late to work or a little extra help on a project, do you think they complained? Or did they only complain when the touch came without extra benefits? When the boss picked them for a TDY but still selected a male counterpart for an award over the woman?"

"Are you saying it's okay to be sexually harassed if you are getting something in exchange for it?" Jackie asked.

"No, I'm saying it wasn't called harassment when there was an exchange. There weren't as many complaints. Wait, I take that back. The guys complained, but then they were accused of being pigs for saying women were taking advantage of their sexuality."

Jackie leaned back in her chair, totally worn out by the barrage the major was throwing at her. Some of it really hit home. She remembered seeing some women turn on the femininity when it was convenient. It always sickened her.

"What's the difference between the old-fashioned idea that the man makes the first move and an advance that is harassment? In my experience, if the guy is good looking, it isn't harassment; if not . . ." He let his sentence trail off.

Jackie understood his point. She had been on the receiving end and had to admit some advances were more welcome than others—and a lot of that depended on how interested she was in the man. But Jackie also knew how to handle herself in unusual situations.

In Korea, guys had hung centerfolds up in the vault. Instead of making a formal complaint, as would have been justified by the regulations, she chose to beat the guys at their own game by hanging her own male art. Not only had that diffused the situation, but it also won her the respect of many of the pilots in the unit. To her, that was much more important than getting a few guys in trouble. They were young and stupid. Everyone makes mistakes, and they should have the chance to learn from them, instead of having their career ruined.

The fine line was hard to draw. Should she have reported the lieutenant who got pushy with her at Whiteman? He stopped when she said no, but she had to put up a fight. What if he hadn't stopped?

"But it's terrifying to come forward and report. The experience is," she cleared her throat, ". . . indescribable."

"No doubt, and we should help those people. But how do we sort out the people who really have an issue and need help, and those who are taking advantage of the political optics?"

Chapter 11

The major's words were still ringing in her ears as she waited for her next appointment to arrive.

Jackie had seen cases thrown out where women had been assaulted, but their prior history of using sexual attention to their benefit had made the jury doubt the testimony.

She knew women who used their femininity to advance themselves or to get out of trouble. She hated to see it happen, but then the women complained it was a man's Air Force, and men had all the advantages because of their sex. Why shouldn't women use the advantage they were given?

That was a double-edged sword, and now it was starting to cut both ways. Too many people were getting hurt in the process.

When her next interviewee knocked at the door, Jackie stood, introduced herself, and had Staff Sergeant Gomez take a seat.

"Thank you for coming in." Jackie sat and folded her hands in her lap.

"I thought the case was closed," Gomez said.

"It is. I'm doing some follow-up, that's all."

"Why are you talking to me and not Sally?"

"Sergeant Adams is in the middle of a move. I left a message for her to call when she reports to her new duty station. Do you keep in touch?"

"No. She kind of ghosted everybody when things heated up. I only saw her at mandatory squadron functions." Gomez picked at her fingernails, not looking at Jackie.

"I see from your statement that you didn't feel Technical Sergeant Perrette was capable of the sexual harassment he was accused of."

"No way, ma'am. He is super professional all the time. He even has a girlfriend."

Jackie raised an eyebrow. "Having a girlfriend doesn't mean he can't harass someone else."

"Of course not. I just meant I've seen them together. She comes to squadron events. They're so cute together."

"What made you so sure he didn't harass Staff Sergeant Adams?"

"I've been around Sergeant Perrette a lot. We've even deployed together. He's never shown any signs of interest in anyone besides his girlfriend. Like, they say this harassment happened five months ago, right? Then why was Sally so nice to him at the squadron picnic less than a month later? We were playing horseshoes, and she was as nice to him as she was to everyone else. If someone had harassed me, I'd be mad as hell." Gomez stopped short. "Pardon my language, ma'am."

Jackie gave a small smile and motioned for her to continue.

"It's just, well, if Sergeant Perrette was really that kind of guy, I can't believe so many people would look up to him. He wasn't even mad at Sally after the report was filed. He acted like everything was normal. He didn't treat her any differently than before."

Jackie was relieved to hear that. The charges had been thrown out for lack of evidence, but simply going through the investigation had to be stressful enough to annoy anyone.

"We need more guys like Perrette. Not those blowhards who still think it's a man's Air Force."

Jackie smiled at that. "You should have seen what it was like twenty years ago. We've made progress."

"But still!" Gomez's eyes flashed, and her hands tightened into fists. "I thought the only enemy I'd be fighting was the one shooting at us. I can't believe we have to be on guard against the people who are supposed to have our backs. If I had known how often women get sexually assaulted in the Air Force, there's no way I would have joined."

"I understand where you're coming from, but you have to remember, the military is representative of the general population. If anything, I would guess our numbers are lower than in the civilian world."

"How can you say that? There are stories in the news all the time."

"That's because of congressional oversight; the Department of Defense must track and report the number of sexual assault and sexual harassment cases to the world. The civilian population doesn't have that same reporting requirement, so those numbers tended to get buried."

"I didn't think of that."

"If anything, I would say, because of the annual training we give, the number of incidents is dropping. More people recognize the signs and stop the situation before it gets out of control. But there's a lot more work to do."

Jackie started the long commute home from Andrews. The last interview had yielded the same results as the previous one. Perrette was well loved and a good NCO. *So where did the accusation come from?*

A horn blared, causing her to jump as she whipped her head around, looking for signs of danger. It was just another impatient driver, taking his anger out on the cars near him. She tried to calm the beating of her heart with slow, deep breaths.

She hated this drive. Her apartment was a quick bus ride away from the Pentagon, and she was able to leave her car parked most of the week. Andrews wasn't on the bus route though, so she had to venture into DC traffic. Exiting I-395, she joined the other commuters heading into Shirlington.

At home, she dumped her backpack on the couch and kicked off her shiny black shoes. Relief that she had a weekend to herself buoyed her spirits, and she poured herself a glass of Riesling from an open bottle in the refrigerator.

Removing the pins that held her hair off her collar, she carried the wine into her bedroom. As she unbraided the rope of hair, her cell phone rang.

"Alison! It's about time you called. How's my niece or nephew?"

"This child is going to be more trouble than you were," her sister said.

"Not sure that's possible. What did the doctor say?"

"She said everything looks good. Even though I'm high risk because of my age, things are going fine."

"Forty is the new thirty. You'll be terrific," Jackie reassured her. Alison was in great shape, and Jackie had full confidence that her sister would do whatever it took to keep her baby healthy.

"Hey! I'm only thirty-nine, thank you very much."

"Even better! Everything will go smoothly. I know it." She was happy for her sister and excited to be an aunt, although she couldn't help but feel slightly cheated that her opportunity to be a mother had died with Stan. Now she would have to live vicariously through her sister and spoil her niece or nephew rotten.

"I'm glad the baby didn't act up during your ceremony. The

doctor said I was right on the border of not being allowed to travel, but there was no way we were missing your promotion."

"It wouldn't have been the same without you," Jackie said. "When is Mom getting to North Carolina?"

"I'm trying to put her off until after the baby's born. She's so excited though, she'd move in tomorrow if I let her."

Jackie laughed. "I wonder if Dad would have anything to say about that."

"It'd give him a little peace, I think," Alison said.

The girls had always been close with their mother, but it wasn't until Jackie joined the Air Force that she started to feel any kind of connection to her father. His drinking had been a problem when they were young. He didn't quit until she and Alison were out of the house. Jackie suspected her mother finally gave him an ultimatum.

Jackie wasn't letting her guard down. He had quit before, only to pick up a bottle again at the worst possible times. Anything could trigger him . . . or nothing.

Alison had forgiven their dad and tried to concentrate only on his good side, but forgiveness wasn't as easy as Alison pretended it to be. Jackie didn't want to say anything to upset her tenuous outlook.

"I can't wait to see Dad hold a baby," Jackie said. "Or change a diaper!"

"Don't hold your breath. I can't imagine Dad changing diapers. I think Mom always did that at our house. I'll just be happy to see Lance change the baby."

"What are you talking about? Lance is as excited about the baby as you are. Didn't you say he helped pick out the decorations for the nursery?"

"I think that was so I wouldn't overspend."

Jackie laughed. "No way. He's almost as quick to share details of the pregnancy with me as you are. When he first felt the baby kick, he was over the moon. I'm sure he'll be just as involved after the baby arrives."

"He is pretty wonderful."

They were quiet for a moment as each woman fell into her musings. Images of Stan on their wedding day, then standing at the bar in a flight suit with a drink in his hand, crooked grin on his face, flashed before Jackie.

"What are you doing this weekend?" Alison finally asked.

Jackie put the phone on speaker as she continued to change out of her uniform. "Nothing. I'll probably visit the Smithsonian Natural History Museum tomorrow and jog around the mall on Sunday. What about you?"

"Your idea of nothing and mine are very different." Alison laughed. "I'll probably get a pedicure and then binge watch a romcom."

"Yeah, I don't think I can sit still that long."

"I'm going to sit while I can. I have a feeling relaxing isn't in the cards for me after this one comes."

"That's why your favorite sister will be there to help. My boss has already approved my leave. She knows I'm waiting on the exact date, and I plan on getting there after you've been home a few days. I don't want to overwhelm you."

A male voice sounded in the background. "Lance is home so I'm going to go. Do a little extra running for me this weekend," Alison said.

The sisters said their goodbyes, and Jackie went to the kitchen to see about dinner. She opened the cupboard and spied a box of Frosted Flakes. Her stomach flipped over. She didn't really care for the sugary cereal but had put it in her cart automatically last time she went to the store. It had been Stan's favorite, and they could never keep enough in the house for him. When she realized what she had done at the checkout, she was too embarrassed to put it back.

She pushed it aside, reaching for the granola behind it. Yogurt and granola had been a favorite breakfast food for her when they lived in Germany. Now, eating alone, it was her go-to for ease and speed. Carrying her dinner into the living room, she clicked on the television and flipped through the various channels without anything catching her eye. Her fingers were itching to open her computer.

Before she had taken her first bite, her phone buzzed. She checked it reflexively, scrolling through the findings the analyst sent her.

Maybe she would go into the office after all.

Chapter 12

Lights popped on like flash bulbs as Jackie triggered the motion sensors on the way to her office. The typically dark halls of the Pentagon loomed beyond the fluorescent reach of the nearest overhead fixture. Looking down a few side corridors as she passed, she noticed other lights were on. She wasn't the only one in the building on a Saturday afternoon.

She unlocked the outer door to the SAPR office, closing the door behind her before making her way to her cubicle, where she booted up the computer. While she waited, she flipped through the papers left for her when she was at Andrews on Friday. Scribbling her signature on a few forms, she cleared away the easy items. Others would take more time to review.

Her email came up, and she reread the analysis comparing Webster's units to other similar units. As she suspected, the numbers of complaints of sexual harassment and assault in units Webster commanded were high, although no complaints had been filed against him.

But here was something interesting. The number of transfer requests out of his units was also much higher than normal. It made sense—one would expect people who were being harassed to want to transfer away from their harasser, whether it was substantiated or not. However, in the case of Webster's units, the requests were disproportionately higher than the number of cases filed. She shot an email to Renko, asking him to locate where some of the transfers were stationed now. Maybe she should also talk to a few who weren't mentioned in the case files and see if it was simply coincidental.

In the meantime, she could start with the names in the reports. Opening a new document on her computer, Jackie made a list of transferees, then searched in the personnel database to find their current duty station and unit. Webster was on his third command now, so the list wasn't short. A few people had already separated from the military, so reaching out to them might be harder. Some left home phone numbers, but she would have no way of knowing for sure if those numbers were still good until she made the calls.

Her stomach rumbled. Glancing at her watch, she decided to treat herself to food at the Pentagon City Mall before catching the bus back to her apartment. She hit print on her list of contacts and tucked the sheet into her pocket. It might be easier to catch the people who had left the military on the weekend when they were more likely to be home than at work.

Jackie was on her fourth call of the evening. It was refreshing that these people didn't hold back. Having already completed their military commitment, they didn't have to worry about backlash from their superiors for speaking candidly about their experiences.

There was certainly no love lost for Lieutenant Colonel Webster. Both men and women said he seemed to be a personable commander, but when he got an idea stuck in his head, nothing would shake him.

"It was like he *wanted* me to have been harassed so he could help me," Cindy told Jackie during their call.

Cindy was in Webster's last unit and had elected to separate.

"I was dating a guy in the unit. He wasn't my boss or anything. We worked together, that's all. Eventually, we decided to call it quits. Nothing bad happened; it just wasn't working out. No idea how Webster found out about it. Next thing I knew, I was in his office being drilled." Cindy released a long sigh. "It really sucked because I was going to try for Italy on my next assignment."

"But why did you get out?" Jackie asked.

"My ex found out and thought I made a complaint against him. Then his friends got mad at me too. No one believed me when I told them I didn't make a complaint. It just got to be too much. They were offering early outs to cut down in our career field, so I took it."

Jackie fought to keep her anger at bay. A woman's career was ruined based on miscommunication and judgment. She inhaled deeply and disguised her indignation with professionalism. "Is there anyone else you think I should talk to?"

"Once you get to the bottom of this, I would love for you to set my ex straight. It was pretty shitty how we ended things."

Jackie took down his name and rank and promised to look him up.

It was getting late, so Jackie decided to hold off on more calls until tomorrow. As she looked back over her notes, key words jumped out at her.

Pressure.

Insistence.

Retaliation.

Chapter 13

Monday morning came quickly, especially because it started with a seven-thirty meeting with the secretary of the Air Force and all the top generals. It was brief but immediately followed by three back-to-back meetings where Jackie was sitting in for her boss.

She made a mental note to be nicer to the general on Mondays.

When she finally made it back to her desk, she only had a few moments to reflect on the rest of the calls she had made on Sunday before the analyst stopped by.

"Good morning, ma'am. Was the information I sent over helpful to you?"

"It was exactly what I was looking for, Ed, thanks. Did anything jump out at you?"

"The number of separations from Webster's unit were outside the range for a unit that hadn't deployed recently."

"Six separate cases in one unit in a year are the highest number across the Air Force, regardless of unit size. Maybe the man is seeing ghosts."

"What do you mean?" Jackie gestured for Ed to sit.

"There must be a reason for the spikes. Can he see things others can't? Or is he seeing things that don't really exist? Have you talked to him yet?"

"No. I wanted to get some background before I tipped my hand. I probably won't get a chance until next week when the boss is back. This is something I want to do face-to-face."

"I don't blame you."

"I did run into him in the hall when I was leaving the JAG's office at Andrews last week. He doesn't seem very imposing," Jackie said.

"Maybe that's why people feel comfortable talking to him," Ed offered.

A knock at her cubicle caught Jackie's attention.

"Ma'am, time for your next meeting," Polk said.

She glanced at her watch. Sergeant Polk managed the office very well. Jackie understood why the general valued him so much.

Jackie and Ed rose. "I'd like to hear how it goes with Lieutenant Colonel Webster, ma'am. This is going to be interesting," Ed said.

Her next meeting, a preparation meeting for briefing the secretary of the Air Force so she could turn around and brief Congress, nearly bored her to tears. She hated wasting time she could be spending investigating Webster or looking into the case Chaplain Vandesteeg had brought her.

Jackie thought working in the Pentagon would be exciting, a place where problems were solved, and innovations approved; she had been naïve. She was quickly realizing she wasn't interested in playing the higher politics of it all. There were so many meetings, she didn't know how anyone got anything done.

She didn't sit down at her desk again until late in the afternoon. Then she logged into the case management system to see if anything had come in from McGuire about Sergeant Davies's case. Nothing yet. She'd make a phone call in the morning to the SARC at the base to see what was going on.

～

The alarm on Jackie's watch went off, reminding her about soccer practice. If she didn't leave right away, she'd be late. The traffic to that side of town was horrible at this time of day.

Grabbing her gym bag, she ducked into the restroom to change before heading to the bus. During the thirty-minute commute, she scrolled through her email and answered whatever questions she could, then checked her schedule for the next day.

By the time the bus stopped near the park, Jackie was ready to let go of the office and focus on the kids. As usual, some parents were waiting on the coaches, chatting with heads together while their kids played on the nearby swings. Jackie waved at the adults and was considering joining them when Leon pulled up.

She detoured to his truck and helped him unload as Vicki ran off to get a few minutes on the playground.

"How was work?" he asked.

"Same shit, different day."

"I get that. Feels like that in OSD too. The only thing that makes it worthwhile is the overseas trips for NATO meetings." Leon had landed a choice assignment as a NATO staff officer working for the secretary for defense.

"It's like you're trying to make me jealous. Are you sure you don't need someone to carry your bags?" Jackie asked, only half joking.

Leon laughed. "I wish I was important enough to have my own aide."

"Well, until you are, my offer to take care of Vicki while you're away still stands."

"You have no idea how much I appreciate that. My parents usually jump at the chance, but they can't always swoop in to rescue me when Sarah is TDY. I'll be glad when her six-month rotation is over." Leon's wife was a C-17 pilot deployed to Afghanistan.

"Speaking of trips, I went to Andrews the other day." Jackie carried the equipment bag to the field and dropped it next to the bench.

His eyes cut a curious look her way. "How'd that go?"

Jackie shrugged. "Not as bad as I thought it would be. A little rough at first, but once I started working, I forgot about everything else."

"What are you working on?"

"There's an unusually high number of cases being filed in one unit there. I think something's up with the commander."

"How so?"

"An airman came to me. Seems the commander twisted her words and now she's stuck in the middle of an assault case."

"Wait? How does that happen?"

"She says she wasn't assaulted but the commander says she was."

Leon stared at her in disbelief. "That doesn't even make sense."

"I know. He won't listen to her and filed an unrestricted report, so now there's an investigation. And she isn't the only one who's telling me he's got his own way of doing things." Jackie placed one foot on the bench and retied her sneaker.

"What an asshole. What are you going to do?"

"I'm not sure yet. Right now, I'm gathering information. If something turns up, I'll take it to the wing commander." Jackie stopped abruptly. Thinking of Dellinger's green eyes sidetracked her train of thought.

She turned away from Leon, busying herself emptying the equipment, but she felt him watching her.

Before he had a chance to ask anything else, a few more parents arrived with their kids.

"Coach Jackie!" The little girl with the scraped knee ran up to Jackie. "Coach Jackie, look at my new Band-Aid! Isn't it cool?"

"Wow, is that Mirabel from *Encanto*?"

"Yeah! She's my favorite." With that, the girl turned and raced back toward the other kids, narrowly avoiding hitting the woman coming up behind her.

"Thanks for taking such good care of her. She won't stop talking about how amazing Coach Jackie is." The woman had a brilliant smile and a slight accent Jackie struggled to place. "I'm Veronica. It's nice to meet you."

Someone called out and Veronica waved. Turning back to Leon and Jackie, she said, "I can't thank you two enough for tiring them out. It makes our evenings much quieter."

Leon and Jackie laughed.

"I can't claim it's entirely selfless. I needed a way to run out Vicki's energy too. She's much easier to put to bed on practice days," Leon admitted.

"Either way, we really appreciate it. Anyway, I'll let you get started." Veronica smiled and left to sit with the parents in the stands.

Leon blew his whistle, and the kids scurried to line up in front of him. When they were all in place, he started singing their warm-up song. As if he were the pied piper, the children followed him in a slow jog around the field, repeating the words he sang. On the last note, they all sprinted to the goal post, racing to be first.

Leon's daughter ran to Jackie. "Coach Jackie, can I pass out the balls?"

"Of course. Thank you for offering." She opened the net bag, allowing the balls to bounce free.

"Kendra's going to help me."

The dark-haired girl with the Mirabel Band-Aid giggled as she tried to catch the bouncing balls.

A few of the boys rushed in, grabbing at the soccer balls. "Wait your turn!" Vicki scolded.

She quickly and efficiently had the kids lined up as she and Kendra passed out the balls for the first drill.

Jackie elbowed Leon. "I wonder where she gets her leadership experience from."

He held up his hands. "That's all her mother. How do you think she keeps me in line?"

"But her angry face when someone takes the last fruit snack—" Jackie turned to Leon, scrunching her nose and pursing her lips. "That's all you!"

Chapter 14

Jackie sat stiffly in her service dress uniform, aware that slouching would wrinkle her pressed appearance. Major Wilson from the legislative liaison office was dressed in a coat and tie for their trip to the Hill. The liaisons were supposed to blend in with the civilians on Capitol Hill, allowing the formal military uniforms to stand out and look that much more impressive when the officers visited.

This wasn't her first trip to meet with a staffer, but Jackie listened intently as the major brought her up to speed on the things happening in the congressman's district. Knowing what military issues he might be concerned with would keep Jackie from being caught off guard if the representative decided to throw something off topic at her. She was also curious to hear why he had an interest in this particular case.

"The congressman knows the father of Staff Sergeant Kirkson, the accused. Kirkson's mother is the one who is pushing the congressman to get involved," the major explained.

"Let me guess. They donate to his re-election campaign?"

"Or at least he hopes they will if he helps them out. That's likely."

Jackie shook her head in disbelief. "I got an update from Wright-Pat. They have witnesses to his pushy behavior. Sergeant Kirkson isn't even fighting it much. His military defense lawyer is trying to blame it on alcohol. Kirkson had too much to drink and didn't stop when he should have. He's asking for leniency but not dismissal."

"If that's in the official record, that's all you need to tell the staffer. Most of the time, the congressman just wants to be able to tell his constituents that he did everything he could to help. They aren't that worried about the outcome. Ready to go?" The major stood and buttoned his suit coat.

"Let's get this over with." She had so many other things she could be working on.

They caught the shuttle bus from the Pentagon to the Hill, Wilson guiding Jackie to the right office. After waiting thirty minutes for the staffer to "tie up some things," they were led into a small conference room.

A man in his early twenties bustled into the room and offered Jackie his hand. "I'm Charlie. Sorry for the wait. The congressman is leaving on a trip, and we've been prepping him."

"No problem. I understand." Inside, Jackie was seething that this young-nothing was entitled to the military respect of a general officer. His shirt was half untucked, and he desperately needed a haircut and a shave.

She listened as he rattled off his insincere concern about a constituent he knew nothing about. She then shared what she had received from the base.

Charlie stood. "Well, I'll let the congressman know, and we'll get back to you if he has any more questions."

The man was gone before Jackie had a chance to push in her seat.

"That went well," Major Wilson said.

Jackie shot him a nasty look. "And why couldn't that have been handled with an email or a phone call? I wasted an afternoon on this trip."

"Sometimes they just need that little stroke that shows them they have the power."

She barely stopped herself from rolling her eyes. "I'm so glad I don't have your job. I couldn't deal with this every day."

"Some parts are better than others, ma'am."

"Like what?"

"When particular wording works its way into legislation—something I advocated for. It makes me feel like what I'm doing makes a difference. What about you? Do you like your job?"

She took her time formulating a response. "We address a big problem most men haven't even acknowledged yet. I want people in the Air Force to be more respectful to each other overall. What I do only addresses the most basic steps. We have a long way to go."

Chapter 15

The next few days were a blur of meetings about meetings. It wasn't until Friday that Jackie was able to reach the SARC at McGuire.

"Ma'am, I'm not sure why your office is involved in this case at all."

"It's a sexual assault case, isn't it?" Jackie asked.

"Not necessarily. We haven't determined yet if it's a legitimate complaint or not," First Lieutenant Ellen O'Connor said.

"That's not your job." Jackie was irritated at the tone the lieutenant was taking with her. "You are to take in the information, get the victim the assistance she *or he* needs, and pass it on to the proper authorities to investigate."

"With all due respect, ma'am, it sounds like he has been talking to the chaplain, so he is getting *help*."

"Why don't I see the report in the case management database?"

The lieutenant sighed. "I was getting ready to put it in, then Sergeant Davies called me and said he wasn't sure he wanted to make a formal complaint."

"Why do you think he changed his mind?"

"No telling. Perhaps he realized his story was getting a little too much attention, and it wasn't what he was looking for."

Jackie got to the count of eight, taking in deep breaths.

"Ma'am? Are you still there?"

"Lieutenant, I think you are in need of some remedial training. I will be in touch with your commander to get it scheduled. Get the report entered by the end of the day." Jackie resisted the urge to slam the phone.

This situation identified a huge hole in their training plan—for SARCs and the general population. Too much emphasis was placed on women as victims and not enough of what happened when the roles were reversed.

She scribbled some ideas in her notebook. As she tried to decide who to assign to revamp their curriculum, she realized the only men in their office were analysts. She never gave it much thought before. This would have to be a discussion point with the general upon her return.

Jackie would be glad to hand the reins of the office—and all the meetings—back to her boss on Monday.

Someone cleared her throat, and Jackie looked up. "I'm sorry. I didn't see you. Can I help you with something?"

The technical sergeant twisted the lanyard holding her building pass in her hands. "I heard you are talking to people in Colonel Webster's squadron about—" She cleared her throat again. "Sexual assault cases."

Jackie waved the woman into a chair in front of her desk. "I am. Did you want to talk to me about it?"

The woman sat with her back straight. She licked her lips. "Colonel Webster is a great man and an even better commander. I'm not sure what you're trying to do, dragging all this up."

Jackie's eyes flicked to her nametag. "Sergeant Buckley, are you in Colonel Webster's squadron?"

She shook her head. "Not now. He was my flight commander at my first duty assignment. He's the only reason I'm still in the Air Force."

Jackie waited for her to continue.

"My superintendent had always been a bully. He was known for it. The officers didn't seem to care because he got his job done, and our inspections were outstanding." Her face twisted in disgust. "His punishments for messing up were always unique. If you couldn't take it, your next duty would be hell.

"One day, he had me walking the line—basically marching back and forth across the parking lot. It was late at night but still above ninety degrees. I was in full gear, sweating like a pig. He finally told me I could take off my flak jacket and helmet. After that, he told me to keep going. I picked up my training rifle to start marching again, and he told me no. He told me to keep taking off my clothes."

Tears ran down her face, but she struggled through her story. "Of course I refused. Then he got in my face and gave me a direct order. I still remember the stink of his coffee breath. When I still wouldn't go along with him, he ripped at my clothes."

She was choking back sobs now.

"It's okay. You don't have to say any more," Jackie assured her.

"I need you to understand. After it happened, no one believed me. Or at least they didn't want to do anything about it. The guy was a decorated master sergeant, and people were afraid of him. I think even my commander was a little afraid."

She wiped her tears with the back of a hand. Jackie offered her a box of tissues, and Buckley took a few.

"Captain Webster—he was only a captain then—was new to the unit. He came in about a week after it happened. He said he could tell I was upset about something. Eventually, I broke down and told him. He was furious. At first, I thought he was mad at me. Then he calmed down. He took me to the SARC himself and waited to give me a ride back to my dorm." Buckley's eyes were trained somewhere in the past.

"Everything blew up when he confronted the master sergeant. The sergeant tried to say I was making it up to get out of work details I didn't want to take. The other guys I hung out with in the unit were too new to know anything. They were afraid for their careers if they went up against this guy." Buckley blew her nose and wiped away her tears.

"My life was a mess for months. I couldn't sleep; eating made me sick. I was put on probationary status. That just made me feel like I was getting raped all over again."

Jackie cringed at the thought.

"But Captain Webster stood by me. He wouldn't let it go. He practically forced the commander to do something. I don't know what he threatened the commander with, but the master sergeant was finally charged."

When it seemed as if Buckley had said all she needed to say, Jackie asked tentatively, "What happened to him?"

"He went to Leavenworth. Seven years. Dishonorable discharge. Life went on. But Webster kept checking on me, made sure I went to counseling. He's a good man. I just thought you should know."

"No one is saying he isn't a good man," Jackie said.

"Why are you investigating him?" She wiped the tears one last time then balled the tissue into her fist.

Jackie stared over the woman's head, trying to pull the right words from the air. "I'm not really investigating him. I'm just asking some questions. He seems to pick up on a lot of these cases, both assault and harassment. I'm trying to figure out how he knows."

"People trust him. He's empathetic and he listens. That's what makes him such a good commander. We need more like him."

Buckley's fervor unsettled Jackie a bit.

"And I hope to harness those traits and use them to train other leaders."

The cold stare coming from Buckley screamed disbelief. She stood. "I said what I came to say. If you need any more information from me, please reach out. I'm stationed here in the building, in security."

Jackie exchanged business cards with her. "If you have anything else you want to tell me, please stop by again or give me a call."

~

It had been a long day and Jackie was looking forward to putting on her comfy sweats and crawling under the covers. As she put the key in her lock, the stomping of running feet inbound spun her around.

"There you are! Don't you ever check your phone?" Bubbling and bursting with energy, Jackie's neighbor practically bounced on her toes. With her long legs and slender arms, she could have been a ballerina. Her curly, dark hair sprang along with her movements.

"Hey, Theresa. Sorry. I've been meaning to text you, but I've been super busy at work."

"When aren't you busy at work? That's your excuse for everything. You promised you'd come out with us. My girlfriends are dying to meet you. I told them all about the bad-ass lieutenant colonel who lives in my building."

Jackie gave her a weak grin. Theresa Cansler had been the first neighbor to welcome Jackie when she moved in, and Jackie was glad for the camaraderie of another professional woman her age. Theresa had filled her in on the highlights of the area and told her how to avoid the tourist traps.

"I'm really exhausted. Can we do it another time?"

"Come on. Just one beer. You'll catch your second wind."

Jackie shook her head. "Next time, I promise."

"I'll hold you to it." Theresa backed away, working in a few dance steps as she did. "The guys of DC are waiting for you." Finishing with a spin, she disappeared around the corner.

Chapter 16

On Saturday, Jackie rode her bike to soccer practice. She got in a good workout and was able to maneuver around much of the annoying traffic that she would have been sitting in had she driven. Leon waved at her when she rolled in. Only he and Vicki were there so far, and they had already set up the cones for the first drills.

"Looks like Vicki is taking over as assistant coach. I knew you didn't really need me."

"We need you, Coach Jackie. Please don't quit." Vicki grabbed Jackie's arm.

Jackie knelt and hugged her. "I'm not going anywhere. I was just teasing your dad."

Other kids arrived, and Vicki was soon distracted with a game of tag.

"What was that all about?" Jackie asked Leon.

He sighed. "Sarah got extended. She won't be home in time for Vicki's birthday like she had planned."

"Ouch. That's gotta suck for both of them."

"And me! Does it make sense that I miss Sarah even more now that we have Vicki? We used to go TDY all the time, and I didn't think anything about it."

"Of course. I'm sure playing the single parent takes a lot out of you."

"I'm counting down the days until her return." Leon made a dramatic grab at his heart.

Jackie threw a ball at him. "Get out on the field. It'll take your mind off it."

While they'd been talking, the team had wandered onto the field. Leon blew his whistle, and the kids came running. Jackie looked around to ensure there were no stragglers. She spotted someone in the tree line at the edge of the park. Assuming one of the kids was still hiding from the seeker in an earlier game, she walked that way.

As she got closer, the figure grew taller, and Jackie realized it wasn't a child, but rather an adult who had been crouched down. A cold sweat broke out on her forehead.

I'm safe. I'm safe. Jackie repeated the mantra over and over to calm her racing heart. Chaplain Vandesteeg had given her various techniques to employ when old fears crept up on her.

Pushing the unfounded anxiety aside and feeling more than a little embarrassed, she gave a little wave and turned back to the field. When she looked over her shoulder, the figure was walking away.

Chapter 17

The following week, Jackie was true to her word. She gave Major General Varn breathing room instead of charging into her office first thing Monday morning. It was late afternoon before her boss sent for her to discuss the past week's events.

"Thanks for covering, Jackie. LL says you did a good job on the Hill."

This time, Jackie couldn't hold back the eye roll.

Major General Varn stifled a laugh. "I understand how you feel, but you have to play the game if you want to get anything done."

"Why? Why can't we just jump to the getting-things-done part? Why do we waste so much time on unimportant things?"

"So they will help us when it is important," her boss explained. "You've seen the musical *Hamilton*, right?"

Jackie nodded.

"This is how the sausage gets made. Help them look good for their voters, and we might get a more positive result on something we want for the Air Force."

Jackie brushed off nonexistent lint from her uniform, averting her eyes. "I reached out to OSI at Wright-Patterson to let them know the Kirkson case had LL attention. I asked them to keep me updated if anything pops up so we can stay in front of it with the congressman."

"Good thinking. Tell me about the McGuire case," her boss said.

Beginning with her concern that the McGuire SARC wasn't taking the case seriously enough, Jackie went on to highlight the problem in their own office of the lack of male representation.

Major General Varn swiveled her chair back and forth in small movements. "You have a point. We'll have to consider that next time a position comes open. In the meantime, we'll just have to be sensitive to it. What do you want to do about the SARC?"

"I held off calling her commander until I had a chance to talk to you. It's probably time to audit their program. We haven't been there in the last two years."

"Go ahead and set that up. I have a feeling this case is going to get a lot of attention." Varn sighed. "Circle back with the LL office. I don't want to highlight this SARC problem to the representative yet, but LL needs to know, just in case. McGuire is a major part of the congressman's portfolio, and we want to stay in front of this."

"We also need to look over all our training to ensure there's no bias toward gender," Jackie offered.

"Absolutely. Assign that to someone else. Let me see it when it's ready. And your pet project? How's that going?"

Jackie filled her in on the interviews she had completed at Andrews Air Force Base so far.

"Your instincts were right. This does sound off. Keep digging."

Knowing that was her cue to leave, Jackie returned to her desk.

Senior Airman Nelson was waiting for her.

"Amanda? What brings you here?"

The airman burst into tears.

It wasn't the first time Jackie cursed the cubicle world they lived in at the Pentagon. She closed the flimsy door that only gave the illusion of privacy.

"Amanda, what is it? Are you okay?"

She took a few deep breaths, then spit out an accusation. "I thought you were going to do something about this! You've made things worse!"

Jackie sat in the chair next to Amanda. "What happened?"

"The commander has assigned me desk duty. He says it's for my own good. He's trying to keep me safe." The last part was said with so much sarcasm, Jackie pictured the air quotes.

"I'm sorry this is happening to you. I am trying to get to the bottom of this. Really. It's going to take some time."

"In the meantime, I'm the piranha of the squadron. No one wants to be partnered with me. The guys make nasty comments. Mac and Jason won't talk to me. I don't know what I did." She broke into sobs again.

Jackie passed her the tissue box and stroked her back as she cried.

After Amanda Nelson left, Jackie found she couldn't concentrate on anything. Her mind raced with all the things she wanted to say to a commander who could be so insensitive. She gave up after thirty unproductive minutes and grabbed her hat.

She stopped at Sergeant Polk's desk to let him know she was going to Andrews for the rest of the afternoon.

When she left the office, she discovered Sergeant Buckley pacing in the hall.

"Were you looking for me?" Jackie asked.

"Why would I be looking for you?"

Appalled by the rude tone, Jackie decided not to respond.

As she walked away, Buckley said to her back, "I see my opinion isn't good enough for you."

Jackie turned. "What does that mean?"

"I told you Colonel Webster was a good commander. The best. He saved me when other commanders may have looked the other way."

"I understand you're grateful to him. I'm glad he was there for you, but that has nothing to do with what's happening now."

"You have no idea what kind of trouble you're stirring up." Buckley stood with her feet slightly apart, hands resting on the gear hooked to her belt.

The thought of a cowboy ready for a gunfight crossed Jackie's mind. "I've noted your opinion, but I'm not going to discuss this with you further."

This time when she walked away, Jackie felt like there was a bullseye on her back.

Chapter 18

"Thanks for seeing me on short notice," Jackie said when Lieutenant Colonel Webster met her at his office door.

"I know you, don't I?" he asked, shaking Jackie's hand.

"We literally bumped into each other a few weeks ago in the headquarters building." She took a seat across from Webster's desk.

"Oh, I remember. You were troubled about something. I hope you found someone to confide in."

"I wasn't troubled. I was distracted."

"A lot of women get the two confused."

His condescending attitude riled her more than it should have. Still shaking with irritation after her conversation with Senior Airman Nelson, she got right to the point.

"Are you aware your reportings of sexual harassment and assault are well above average from any other unit in the Air Force?"

Webster leaned back in his chair, nonplussed. "No, I didn't, but thanks for letting me know."

"I wouldn't think that's something to be proud of."

"The fact that the women under my command feel comfortable enough to come forward when there's an incident makes me very proud."

"But I understand you are filing unrestricted reports even when the victim doesn't come forward."

"Who are you referring to?"

"Senior Airman Nelson for one."

He shook his head. "She was too frightened. Someone else came to me on her behalf."

"Who?"

Webster placed his elbows on his desk and clasped his hands together. "Have you ever been a commander, Jackie? I can call you Jackie, can't I?"

He didn't give her a chance to answer. "People come to me in confidence. I can't reveal my sources to satisfy your curiosity."

"As I'm *sure* your executive officer told you, I work for the SAPR office for the secretary of the Air Force. This is not idle curiosity." Jackie's tight smile did nothing to hide her irritation.

"Still." He spread his arms in a helpless gesture, its casual nature in opposition to Jackie's intensity. "What specifically are you here for? A base-level complaint doesn't seem like something you'd be involved in."

"We get involved in *every* case." She shed any semblance of a smile. "We oversee the program to ensure all victims are heard."

"Well, it's good to know Airman Nelson has been heard all the way to the Pentagon."

"I spoke with Amanda. She said she was not raped, as your report claims."

"She's scared of talk around the squadron. It's understandable but it'll die down quickly."

"What proof do you have of the rape? With her denial, there are no witnesses." Jackie willed herself to not rise to his bait.

"You should know better than anyone; in a he-said, she-said case, most jurors believe the woman."

Between gritted teeth, she managed to respond, "But *she* is *not* saying. You are alleging."

"My job is to look after her best interests. Someone was worried enough to come forward on her behalf. I won't let this behavior go uncensored in my unit."

Jackie stared at him in disbelief. There was no getting through to this man.

Chapter 19

"What were you thinking?" Major General Varn's stern face spoke louder than her words.

Jackie felt unsteady, standing at attention in front of her boss's desk. "I—I was trying to get to the bottom of this. Airman Nelson was so upset by the false accusation—"

"And how do you think she's going to feel when her boss calls her into his office again and reams her for going against his word?" Varn cut her off.

Jackie didn't have a response.

"And how is she going to feel if she is asked to testify in court and she has a different story than the one she told you?"

It was hard to meet the disapproval in her supervisor's eyes.

"I was only trying to help," Jackie said weakly.

"Help by doing your job. Gather the facts. Present the facts. Blame is not yours to assign. You're not a detective, no matter how well that's turned out for you in the past."

The blow took the wind out of Jackie, and it must have shown.

"I'm sorry," the general said quickly. "That's not what I meant."

Jackie's legs shook. "May I be dismissed?"

In a much gentler voice, Varn said, "No. Sit down."

She sat, staring at her hands, not trusting herself to look at her boss respectfully.

Varn leaned forward in her chair. "That was uncalled for. I only meant I don't want you to put yourself in a situation where you may be hurt. Don't take any unnecessary risks."

The silence between them grew uncomfortable.

"Go." Varn blew out her breath. "We'll talk again later."

Without even glancing her way, Jackie rose and left the office.

Back at her cubicle, she tried to concentrate on her email inbox, but the walls felt too close and too thin. She needed to step away.

Heading toward the center of the building, she weaved around the slower walkers in the halls. Instead of the elevator, she opted for the stairs as usual, finally pushing open into the courtyard.

After the steady fluorescent lighting of the halls, the brilliant sunshine and clear blue sky released the vice tightened around her lungs. Jackie inhaled deeply and counted to three as she exhaled. She began a stroll around the paths that, like bicycle spokes, fanned out from the center to connect to the rim along the inner Pentagon walls.

This five-square-acre oasis in the center of the largest office building in the world was a hidden treasure. A no-hat, no-salute area, all ranks came here throughout the day to take a break, eat lunch, or get better cell reception. It was Jackie's favorite place to get fresh air in the middle of the city.

As she made the loop along the inner walls, she chided herself for being stupid. The general was right. Jackie had no business going directly to Webster without making sure she had all the facts and had thought through the consequences.

She also had to admit she had been lucky in the past— catching her stalker and finding Stan's killer. Things could have easily turned out very differently.

Now she had to focus on her next move, besides apologizing to Major General Varn for being disrespectful, that is. She needed to finish typing up her notes and crosschecking the interviews she had completed.

Reenergized, Jackie cut down one of the sidewalks laid out like spokes with the Ground Zero Café in the middle and went back to her office.

Jackie hurried to her desk and picked up the phone on the fourth ring.

"Thought you'd want to know, Staff Sergeant Kirkson has a DUI from his training base, and if rumors are to be believed, he deserved a few more, but his mommy made them go away," the OSI agent from Wright-Patterson explained.

"That's insane!" Jackie slumped into her seat and grabbed a pen to take notes.

"Explains why he isn't fighting this too hard. His new defense lawyer—now civilian, not military, by the way—is trying to plea bargain his way out of a court martial."

"I'll bet he is," Jackie said. "Is the JAG going for it?"

"He's listening. If the airman will take an Other Than Honorable discharge, it might go away."

"Does that put him on the sex offenders' registry?"

"Not sure about that one. It probably depends on what charge they use. If they drop it to conduct unbecoming, I doubt it. I can't imagine his mother will let her son be labeled for life."

"Thanks for the update. I'll contact LL."

Jackie hung up the phone and typed out a quick email to Major Wilson with the update. She knew this was going to drive another visit, and she dreaded it.

Then, not wanting to put it off any longer, Jackie dialed the number for the Andrews wing commander.

"Sir, first, I have to apologize. I handled the situation poorly." Jackie held her breath while she waited for his reaction.

"That's one way to put it," Colonel Dellinger said, but he didn't sound angry.

"It won't happen again."

"You shook Webster up. He tried to act put out by it, coming in here with his bluster and complaints about being accused of something. But I could tell he was just trying to get ahead of the shit storm."

Jackie suppressed a smile.

"I did my part and gave your general a call, but I also let Colonel Webster know we would be taking a closer look at the SAPR cases in his unit. You may want to steer clear of him for a while. He's none too happy."

"Yes, sir. Thank you for allowing me to go forward with this."

"I wouldn't be much of a commander if I didn't listen to those who are experts in their fields. General Varn thinks a lot of you, and I have great respect for her."

Jackie's face flushed.

"I'd appreciate it if you'd keep me in the loop." Jackie thought she heard a smile in his voice.

Or perhaps that was wishful thinking.

The usual cacophony from so many voices in the food court made this the liveliest room in the Pentagon. Jackie and Leon snagged a table on the outer edge alongside the windows into the courtyard. As Leon dug into his sandwich, Jackie picked at her food.

"What's bugging you?" he asked between mouthfuls.

"I got my ass chewed. Now I'm trying to figure out my next steps."

"By who? Varn? I wouldn't want to cross her."

"Yeah. Apparently, I got a little ahead of myself by talking to Webster." She took a forkful of her rice.

"Talked to him about what?"

She moved restlessly in her seat. "I think something fishy is going on in his squadron. There are too many sexual assault and harassment charges for it to be normal."

"And you're trying to figure it out? Isn't that part of your job?"

"I thought so. Guess Varn thinks I should leave it to the professionals."

Leon choked on his food when he started laughing. He took a drink and composed himself. "Does she know you at all? You're one of the most professional people I know."

"Maybe, but I'm not a detective—her words."

"Don't the best officers all have a bit of detective in them? We're constantly exploring new options and analyzing the facts to solve problems. You latch on to something and don't let go until you get to the bottom of it. You're more gifted at that than most."

A spark of confidence returned to Jackie, along with extreme gratitude to her friend.

"You aren't giving up, are you?" He finished his sandwich and rolled the wrapping into a ball.

"No way. But Webster rubs me the wrong way. I'm not sure if he's guilty of something or if I just don't like him."

"Doesn't have to be mutually exclusive. What is it about him you don't like?"

"He's patronizing. He tries to come across as compassionate and selfless, but he just thinks he's right all the time—to the point that he doesn't listen when others speak."

"And I know how you are when people don't listen to you." A grin split his face.

She threw her napkin at him, and he batted it away.

"Why is he making these false accusations?" She pushed her food aside and crossed her arms.

Leon looked at her without speaking until she met his eye. "You are going to figure it out. It's what you do."

Chapter 20

"Why are you still here? It's Friday night. Shouldn't you be relaxing?"

Jackie glanced up at Major General Varn's voice and stood. "I still need to get the McGuire files together to hand off to Lieutenant Colonel Cheng."

She hadn't talked to her boss more than necessary since her misstep with Webster. She was giving them both time to cool down after their exchange.

"That was a smart idea, getting your IMA involved," Varn said. The individual mobilization augmentee (IMA) assigned to Jackie's position was a reservist who trained to fill in for Jackie or others in her office in case someone got deployed.

"He needed his two-week annual tour anyway. The timing worked out."

"Is he ready for this on his own?"

"Absolutely. Plus, having a man handle this situation might be better. It'll definitely get the SARC's attention."

"I have something else I want you to handle. We received a call on the helpline. I'd like you to work it personally," Varn said.

"Yes, ma'am. What's the issue?"

"There's a victim at Wright-Patterson who doesn't feel she's being heard. Listen to the recording next week, then give her a call."

"Yes, ma'am."

Varn started to walk away but Jackie stopped her. "I got a call from OSI at Wright-Pat on the Kirkson case." Jackie gave her a quick run-down on what she had learned.

"Did you notify LL?"

"Yes, ma'am."

"Good. Well, don't stay too late. The work will still be here on Monday," Varn said.

"I don't have too much more to do. I'll be gone soon."

As soon as the general left, Jackie picked up her phone and typed in the right combination of numbers to pull up the voicemail to the helpline.

The recording started with a long pause before any words were spoken. "I was told you could help me. My name is Erin Mollner. I'm a staff sergeant at Wright-Pat. I was raped." The caller's voice cracked. She cleared her throat before she went on. "My . . ." More throat clearing. ". . . attacker was caught but . . ." The girl was crying now. "How can he get away with this? He's still in the Air Force. He's still in the squadron! What do I need to do? Please call me on my personal cell, not the office." She gave her contact information and hung up.

Jackie jotted everything down. Then she opened the case management system. She added a call to the Wright-Patterson SARC to her to-do list for Monday. When she saw the name of the accused, she groaned.

Kirkson.

Jackie answered the knock on her apartment door to find a determined Theresa waiting. "No excuses. Let's go."

As Jackie tried to think up a plausible reason why she couldn't go out, Theresa pushed her way into the apartment and plopped down on the couch. Crossing sculpted legs that Jackie would kill for, she said, "I'll wait."

Sighing, Jackie made her way to the bedroom to search for an acceptable outfit. Anything she had would look drab beside Theresa's natural beauty. "There's wine in the frig. Help yourself."

She sifted through her closet, realizing it had been a long time since she had dressed up for any reason. Flipping through her usual fall color outfits, she picked out a more colorful salmon and gold paisley print blouse and a complementing skirt. She slipped on the silky shirt, remembering the last time she had worn this ensemble. It was a birthday party for a friend in Germany. Not wanting to sink into melancholy, she shifted her attention to what to do with her hair.

Five minutes later, Jackie emerged from her bedroom to find Theresa sipping a glass of wine, flipping through a magazine. "You look great! You'll be fighting them off with a stick tonight!"

Theresa stood and handed Jackie the glass of wine she had poured for her. "Drink up. We need to catch the next bus."

The muggy night hinted of rain. Theresa paraded quickly toward the bright lights and blaring music issuing from the nightclub. Jackie trudged along behind, still not sure she wanted to be there. She had ridden the bus past this building many mornings and never noticed it. As they got closer, the flashing lights distorted her vision.

When they entered the bar, they were greeted with cheers and waves from four ladies gathered around a table against the wall. Theresa pushed her way through the crowd of bodies, dragging Jackie by the hand. A pitcher of something was half empty on the sticky table.

While Theresa yelled the introductions over the DJ's music, one of the ladies handed them each a drink. Jackie answered a few polite questions, but then Theresa's friend Anne resumed the tale she had been telling before they had joined them. Jackie was grateful to be able to sit quietly and take in the bar scene.

It was a totally different atmosphere from the Air Force clubs she was used to. The lack of uniforms and nametags made everyone seem like they were in disguise. There was no immediate recognition of rank or unit to be able to determine her place in the pecking order. This left Jackie feeling oddly off kilter.

When the ladies got up to dance, Jackie begged off. She hadn't had enough to drink to loosen up that much. As she watched, her mind replayed the phone message from Erin Mollner, and she practiced the call she had to make next week. She wished she didn't have to wait until after the weekend to get started.

A waitress set a drink down in front of Jackie.

"I didn't order this," Jackie explained.

"He did." The waitress pointed to a clean-cut man in his early thirties sitting at the bar. "He said you looked lonely sitting by yourself."

"Thank him for me but don't encourage him. I'm not interested."

"Got it."

Laughing and shooting playful barbs at each other, the women returned to the table to rehydrate.

"Where'd this drink come from?" Theresa asked.

"Guy at the bar."

"Aren't you going to drink it?" Anne said.

"No. I don't know what's in it."

Anne brought the drink to her lips and downed it without taking a breath. "Lots of vodka, I'd say."

"That was stupid. You don't know him. He could have put something in that drink." Jackie was incensed.

Anne gave a little wave to the man. "I could get to know him."

Jackie shook her head. Theresa and her friends didn't seem at all concerned about their safety. Jackie's mind spun with the potential dangers that drinking in public entailed. Hell, she knew the stories of what could happen drinking on base; she wasn't about to take any chances at a bar where she didn't know anybody.

As the next song started, Theresa grabbed Jackie's hand and tried to drag her onto the dance floor.

"No, I'm fine. I really don't like to dance."

"Come on. You need to cheer up." Theresa shimmied a little to make Jackie laugh.

She chuckled. "I warned you, I'm not much of a party person. You're the one who insisted I come."

"Relax and let yourself go a little. Maybe another drink." Theresa searched for the waitress.

"No, you go dance. Have fun."

"Come on, Theresa. They're playing our song." Anne grabbed Theresa and pushed her way through the crowd, dragging Theresa along.

Jackie squinted at her watch in the dim light. Figuring she had stayed long enough to be polite, she made her way to the door. As she passed the dancers, she made eye contact with Theresa and mimed her intention to go home. Waving, she ducked out before Theresa could come after her.

She flagged down one of the many taxis circling the bars at this time of night and gave an address near her apartment building. She was relieved to close the door on the commotion and merriment. Resting her head on the back of the seat, Jackie's thoughts once again made their way back to Erin's phone call. She needed to find a way to help this young lady and restore her faith in the Air Force. Hell, Jackie needed to restore her own faith in the system who had apparently failed this airman.

Chapter 21

Early Monday morning, Jackie placed a call to the SARC at Wright-Patterson Air Force Base in Ohio.

After she introduced herself, she got down to business. "Can you give me any information about Erin Mollner's case?"

"Did she call you?"

"Yes, she did."

"Good. I told her getting your office involved was the only way we were going to get any traction."

Jackie shifted the receiver to her other hand and reached for a pen. "What's going on?"

"A young female airman was drinking at the party. A male airman walked her to the dorms. He became forceful and didn't take no for an answer."

"Sounds pretty straightforward," Jackie said.

"I agree. And she tested positive for ketamine, a date-rape drug. The commander said he wanted to spare her the indignity of the trial. Rumor has it he is considering an article fifteen with a loss of a stripe."

"That's it?"

"That's it. That's why Erin is so incensed. And she should be! The guy deserves to be in jail, not laughing it up with his buddies at the club."

The pressure built up in Jackie's head, threatening to explode. She tried to think through alternate scenarios or reasoning she may have missed.

"What is OSI saying?"

The SARC sighed. "They're pretty tight-lipped. I know they are doing a thorough investigation. I was with Erin when she gave a list of names to contact for witness statements for the night of the party. A bunch of her friends let Erin know when they had been contacted."

"Did you see the report OSI gave to the commander?"

"I don't even know if they're done yet. Erin's counsel may have a copy."

Jackie made a note to follow up on the findings. "How's Erin holding up?"

"She's pissed now. Obviously, at first, she was horrified. Then she was resigned to the idea she was going to have to testify. When she heard the guy might get an article fifteen, she figured that meant a dishonorable discharge. Then she saw him at work, acting like nothing had happened; she was shaken. She called me in tears. When she tried to talk to the commander, he blew her off. Her counsel couldn't even get answers from him. That's when I suggested she call the Pentagon hotline. I thought maybe some pressure from above would shake things loose."

"I'm glad you had her call. I'm going to reach out to her next. I wanted to have some background before we talked."

The ladies said their goodbyes, and Jackie rested her head in her hands. This felt so much like a good-old-boys coverup that her stomach was queasy.

There was no sense putting off the inevitable. She contacted Erin Mollner.

After Erin added more details to what was provided by the SARC, she asked, "Why isn't he being punished? How can he get away with this?"

Jackie didn't have the answers. "Let me look into it. I'll get back to you as soon as I know something."

She took down the contact information for the victim's counsel assigned to Erin's case. "Can you contact your counsel and let him know what he can release to me with your permission? That will make things easier."

"Sure. I'll have him call you. Anything to get this over with sooner."

"What do you mean, he isn't coming?" Jackie made an effort to keep her voice from rising.

"Something came up. He'll have to reschedule," the staffer said.

The LL officer stood. Jackie stayed in her seat, incredulous. "We've been waiting over an hour."

"It couldn't be helped." The young man who dropped the bombshell left as quickly as he had appeared.

Major Wilson waited patiently for Jackie to gather herself. She gave him a withering look. "Don't come to me when he reschedules. I'm sure I'll be too busy."

She pushed herself out of the chair and threw her bag over her shoulder.

Wisely, Wilson kept his mouth closed as they boarded the shuttle to the Pentagon. Jackie continued to fume. *Another afternoon wasted on political bullshit.*

When she couldn't stand it any longer, she blurted out, "I have people I can really be helping, you know. Instead of ego-stroking bullshit."

"Yes, ma'am."

"Why does this ass get to jerk my chain? Like his time is more valuable than mine?"

"I understand your frustration."

"I thought he was supposed to serve the people. Is this just a power trip for him? See how many people he can jerk around? Is it a game?"

The question didn't really have an answer and they both knew it.

"Do you feel better now?" Wilson asked.

"A bit. Thanks for letting me get that off my chest."

"You aren't the first one, trust me."

"Do you think the congressman will get involved and bail Kirkson out of this?"

Wilson took his time answering. "House representatives are constantly campaigning because the vote is every two years. Olan has held his position for a long time. He's going to be hard to unseat. It may not be worth the political capital."

"How do you keep all this political stuff straight? It hurts my head."

He shrugged with one shoulder. "It's my job."

When he didn't go on, Jackie shook her head.

"Erin doesn't deserve this. She has gone through hell, and a man is playing politics with her life."

"I totally agree."

Stepping out the doors closest to the bus station, she was disconcerted to realize how late it was. Being inside the huge building all day, it was easy to lose track of time. Now the sky was fully dark, except for the bright lights illuminating the two-level bus platforms.

She held out her phone to access her metro card as she got on the bus. No problem finding a seat at this hour. She plopped down and pulled up the eReader app on her phone and tried to lose herself in a good mystery, but her concentration circled back to the sound of Erin's voice.

A few stops later, she got off two blocks from her apartment. Her mind had turned to dinner plans, so it took a moment for her to notice the car creeping along behind her. There were no other cars in this segment of the neighborhood. It was mostly a commuter area. Jackie steered her steps on the sidewalk to carry her further from the street. The car seemed to be keeping pace with her.

Heart pounding and pulse racing, she tried the mantra, *I'm safe. I'm safe.*

Her instincts were having none of that. Sometimes hair raising on the back of your neck was really a warning of bad things to come. With shaking hands, she pulled out her phone as she continued to move quickly toward the safety of her apartment complex.

Glancing over her shoulder, the headlights of the car blinded her, making it impossible to see the driver. Turning on the camera app, she stopped suddenly and pointed her phone lens at the car.

With a squeal of the tires, it sped away. All Jackie could make out was a dark color, maybe blue. She'd check the footage later to see if the camera picked up anything else.

Fighting not to panic, she made a break for her apartment, turning the deadbolt as soon as she was inside.

In the movies, this situation would usually call for whiskey, but Jackie had to settle for white wine. She poured a tall glass and took a long swallow before refilling the glass. Hands finally stilled, Jackie plugged her phone into the computer. With the benefit of the larger screen, she was able to make out the outline of the car. It wasn't anything remarkable—an SUV. She didn't really know cars very well and couldn't even tell if it was blue or black or if the flash of her camera had distorted the color. There was no way to know if the driver had been a man or a woman. The license plate wasn't even readable because of the angle of the shot.

She closed her laptop. It had been a reach, and she had only taken the picture to get the driver's attention. That seemed to have worked. At least they stopped following her.

~

Jackie strained to read what she had scribbled in her notebook so she could transfer the notes into a file on her computer. She added a new sticky note to her monitor, reminding her to follow up on the climate assessment from Andrews. Yanking another yellow square from the screen, she wadded it up and threw it in the trash. The phone rang.

"I hate to tell you this, but Kirkson's backtracking on his story." The OSI agent from Wright-Patterson got right to the point.

"What do you mean?" Jackie asked.

"At first he wasn't fighting it. He admitted he had been drinking, and things got carried away."

"And now?"

"Now his mother's engaged. He's still saying alcohol was involved, but now his story is that it was consensual. They were making out and everything was fine. Someone found out, the young lady got embarrassed, and made up a story."

"What do you think?"

"I can't give you details, but this isn't the first time something like this has happened," the agent said.

"He's been charged with assault before and he's still in the Air Force?"

"Accused, not charged. The other two women recanted their stories. If I was a betting man, I'd say money changed hands."

"That's horrible."

"Young airmen don't make much money. Throw a sizeable amount of cash at them to not have to testify and relive embarrassing moments? My guess is some would see that as the best of a very bad deal. If it's any consolation, he doesn't have a history of beating. It's more like not taking no for an answer."

"Where did Kirkson get that kind of money?"

"Must come from his parents."

Jackie blew out a deep breath of frustration. "Now what?"

"We're not done with the investigation yet, so no charges have been brought. Kirkson's lawyer is already maneuvering. He's trying to make a deal before we get to that point. Seems like he's an expert in that practice."

"Who's he trying to deal with? Kirkson's commander?"

"His boss is a civilian, so his title is director. But, yes, I have a feeling they are talking. The director has called us a few times asking very specific questions."

"But that's not allowed, is it? Isn't that something like obstruction?"

The agent gave a quiet chuckle. "It's not like on TV. Things are never that clear cut. In a perfect world, the commander—or director, in this case—would keep themselves removed so they can make a decision based only on facts presented to them. But we have no recourse if they don't."

The taste of bile rose in Jackie's throat. Her clear sense of right and wrong was constantly challenged at this level in the military. Her time as a lieutenant missile launch officer with a checklist was much easier to navigate.

"Anyway, I wanted to give you a heads up in case you get a call from the Hill," the agent said.

"I hate that politics is even a consideration. Can't we just do right by the victim?" Her sarcasm dripped into the phone.

"That's not the way the world turns, unfortunately."

She had just hung up when her IMA walked in.

"You were right about that SARC office. It's a mess." Lieutenant Colonel Brad Cheng plopped down in a chair in front of Jackie's desk. "It doesn't look like anyone's paying attention, so Lieutenant O'Connor is doing whatever she wants."

"That's what I was afraid of." Jackie opened the file Cheng handed her. The numerous red marks on the inspection checklist stood out like a sore thumb. "Recommendations?"

"Fire the SARC as soon as possible, but you'll need to backfill it right away. They have too many issues to let the position sit empty."

"Maybe some of our reservists could step in. Let's see if we can get the money to bring them on." Reserve days were allocated in the budget but only so many per office could be used above and beyond their two-week annual tour and one weekend a month. Those extra days were in high demand with the ever-shrinking active-duty population.

Jackie leaned back in her seat. "Did you talk to Davies while you were there?"

"Sure did. I think the guy's got a case."

"How does he feel about it?"

"Your man Vandesteeg is a good guy. He's saying all the right things to support Davies. I just think the sergeant needed someone else to validate his claims. He was starting to feel like he had imagined it."

"And now?"

"I would recommend a road trip."

She sighed. Her mind immediately began reorganizing her schedule, cataloging the work she could do on the road and what she would need to hand off.

"Put together some names for me who can whip that office into shape. Let me know how many days I need to get authorized for the reservists to work."

She stood and walked with Cheng to the front of the office.

Sergeant Polk waited until Cheng walked away before

speaking to Jackie. "Major Wilson from LL called. He'd like you to stop by when you get a chance."

"Please let him know he can stop here around three. I'm not going out of my way to do another dog and pony show."

"Will do."

Chapter 22

It didn't take long for Airman Mollner's counsel to get in touch with Jackie.

"What's a normal punishment in a case like this?" Jackie asked.

"With as many character witnesses as we have, other than the victim, it's typically a slam dunk. Usually we don't even go to trial. A lot of people saw them together at the club, and Kirkson escorted her out when she was stumbling."

"What happened on this one?"

"Beats me. The JAG doesn't even have the case from OSI yet. We thought everything was working through the channels, then we heard Kirkson's lawyer is trying to make a deal. He's saying it's so my client doesn't have to testify. But it's a shit deal. They're looking at barely a slap on the wrist."

"What's Kirkson's boss telling you?"

"No one was hurt."

"What?!" The pressure in Jackie's head skyrocketed. Her heart raced, and she was ready to lash out at someone.

"Erin had passed out. She says she was raped but there's no proof. No semen. The DNA from the accused could have easily been transferred from their interaction at the club."

"Can you appeal?"

"There's nothing to appeal. No ruling has been officially made. I made sure the director knew we weren't happy, but at this point, there's nothing we can do. We have to let it play out."

"That's horrible. What other options does she have?"

"She can try it in civil court, but Erin would need to get a civilian lawyer, and the accused's parents have money. They've already hired outside counsel."

"Please keep me in the loop," Jackie said.

"You do the same."

When Jackie hung up the phone, she stood and paced the office. It was bad enough that Erin had to go through the initial assault, now she was dealing with this shit show too. There had to be something else she could do.

A thought struck her. She pulled out her cell phone and logged into a popular social media app.

It didn't take long to find Kirkson's profile. Skimming past the drunk party pictures, she found a few of him posing with an older couple in front of a restaurant. He tagged the people and the restaurant, so Jackie followed the trail.

Lynda Kirkson's social media account was also public. Most of the pictures were of various storefronts and office buildings in Burlington County, New Jersey. Jackie made a list as she scrolled through the posts. She marveled at the number of businesses Lynda seemed to be involved with. *Guess that's where the money is coming from.*

Jackie worked her way down the list, pulling up the websites for each of the businesses on her computer and jotting down addresses. She wasn't sure what the information would tell her, but she felt she had to do something.

Major Wilson knocked on Jackie's cubicle promptly at three.

She looked up from her work and waved him into a chair. "What's up this time?"

"Do you have an investigation going on at McGuire?"

"We probably have several going on. Why?"

"Is it true one of the complainants is a guy?"

The report was unrestricted, so Jackie didn't see any reason to withhold the information. "As a matter of fact, one case does happen to have a male victim."

"A congressional staffer from the McGuire district called. He doesn't like the optics on this one."

"We never like the optics on sexual harassment. What exactly is bothering him about this one?"

"He feels the gentleman may be making accusations for the attention."

Jackie scoffed. "You mean the nasty comments made behind his back but loud enough for him to hear? Or when someone wrote 'bitch' on his car window? That attention?"

Major Wilson shifted uncomfortably. "I'm just reporting on the call I took from the staffer. They want this to go away before the press gets hold of it."

"I don't think you will be able to accurately interpret what I want to say to the staffer." Jackie's voice was tense.

He held up his hands in defense. "I'm the messenger. But, really? Does this guy have a case?"

"He has the right to be heard. If you don't have anything helpful to say, we're done."

"Yes, ma'am." Wilson stood and ambled toward the door.

"Wait."

Wilson turned to her.

"Which congressman?"

"Olan."

"Figures." She waved Wilson away.

On a hunch, she pulled up McGuire Air Force Base on the computer. She slumped back into her seat. It was located in Burlington County, New Jersey.

Chapter 23

Chaplain Vandesteeg wrapped Jackie in a warm hug when she entered his McGuire office late Monday afternoon. It had been years since she had seen him in person, but they had kept in touch after being stationed at Langley Air Force Base together.

"I'm so glad you're here. Sorry it wasn't under better circumstances," the chaplain said.

"I'm sorry too. I shouldn't have waited this long." Jackie looked around the space. "Walls are pretty bare, aren't they?"

"I told you I'm working on retirement. I'm sorting through things a little at a time so I won't feel stressed at the end." He led her back out the door. "Let me show you where you can hang your hat."

He escorted her to a small office at the end of the hall. "Michael Davies will be here soon, but I wanted to give you a few minutes to set up and grab a coffee. Do you need anything?"

Jackie shook her head. "No. Thanks. This is great." She dropped her computer bag and hat on the empty desk.

"Carole is expecting you for dinner, so don't work too late. We'll catch up tonight."

Standing alone in the room, Jackie tried to deal with the flood of emotions threatening to overtake her. She loved Chaplain Vandesteeg, and he had always been there for her, but thoughts of him were tangled up with the loss of her best friend at Whiteman and then Stan's death.

Before she sank into melancholy over the past, she pulled out her notebook with lists of questions and set to work.

When Sergeant Davies came in, she shook his hand and smiled, trying to put him at ease. The dark circles under his eyes were evidence things weren't going well for him.

They sat in the two guest chairs, without the desk between them. She leaned in to demonstrate she was listening while keeping a respectful distance. Part of her wanted to reach out to comfort him but knew that was the wrong move in this situation.

"Lieutenant Colonel Cheng already gave me the details of your report. I'm not going to make you go over that again."

The relief on his face was evident.

"I'm more concerned with how you're doing now. Do you have a support system?"

He shrugged. "I talk to the chaplain regularly."

"What about family?"

"No way. My dad would be embarrassed. A real man wouldn't shy away from a woman's advances."

"Who's that talking right now? You or your dad?"

"Both, I guess. He raised me." Crossing his arms, he tucked his hands into the cavity under his shoulders, like a petulant child.

"Well, if you can't believe in yourself, it's going to be a long road."

Another shrug. "I wish I had never brought it up."

"But if your boss is treating you this way, how many others do you think she has manipulated?"

He threw his hands up in a helpless gesture. "Maybe they don't mind it so much."

"Or maybe they acted like they didn't mind because it was easier than confronting the issue."

Davies remained silent.

"If your female coworker came to you with a complaint similar to yours, what would you do?"

"I assume punching the aggressor's lights out is out of the question."

Jackie gave a small smile.

"I would encourage her to report," Davies admitted.

"So why are you any different?"

"A man doesn't usually complain when a woman hits on him. Besides, guys are usually big enough to stop a woman from any kind of real harm, if it comes to that."

"But aside from the actual inappropriate touching, harassment is more than physical. When a person holds a position of authority, they can affect your career."

"Don't I know it," he mumbled.

"See? That's what I mean. How many other careers do you think she's ruined?"

"Filing the complaint isn't doing me any favors either. No one wants to work with me. They're afraid I may file a complaint against them."

Jackie's frustration broke free. "That's just stupidity talking. They aren't half as brave as you are."

"Easy for you to say. You aren't the one getting the nasty looks or having your desk decorated with pink crepe paper."

Jackie stared out the window as she contemplated how much to reveal.

"I've been in your shoes."

Sergeant Davies's head snapped up. "You have?"

"Yep. I was a young lieutenant on missile crew duty. I didn't report the harassment, but it came to the attention of my squadron commander. When he took me to see the judge advocate, I was warned what the defense would do to my reputation. I was only twenty-five or twenty-six at the time.

Even my dad discouraged me from pursuing charges. He felt I should keep my head down if I wanted to move up in the ranks."

She ran her palms down the top of her thighs to her knees, trying to release some of the tension.

"What did you do?" His voice was almost a whisper.

"I let it drop. I didn't pursue it. I was looking out for myself, not concerned about what happened to anybody else."

She glanced up to meet his eyes. "I have regretted it every day since. In this job, I see what some folks are suffering through. I wonder how much would have changed had I spoken up back then. What if a lot of us had spoken up?"

Davies turned his head. "I hear you. It doesn't make it any easier."

"I understand. But my job is to help you make a decision you won't regret later. And I will support you no matter what you do."

Chapter 24

Yeah, she definitely has an eye for hot guys," Staff Sergeant Green told Jackie as they chatted over coffee at the base food court.

"What do you mean?" she asked.

"Whenever she needs help with a special project, she always calls in one of the guys. When they win an award, she's the one to present it. I won group-level NCO of the quarter last period, and it was presented by my squadron commander. No one from the group even showed up." Green looked at her hands. "I guess it could be a coincidence, but it sure does happen a lot."

"What do you think about Sergeant Davies's claims of sexual harassment?" Jackie asked.

Green swirled the last of the coffee in her cup. "I guess it could be true. It wouldn't surprise me. I'm just shocked that he reported it. I mean, really, what guy turns down that kind of attention?"

When Jackie stayed silent, Green finally met Jackie's eye, then she sat straighter in the chair. "Ah, I mean . . . not that she has any right to treat anybody that way."

"You really need to think about what you just said. If Sergeant Davies was a woman, would you say the same thing?"

"Well, no, that's not what I meant . . ."

Jackie let her stew a few minutes more. "Thank you for agreeing to talk to me today. I appreciate your candor."

Green rose. "Yes, ma'am. I'm sorry, ma'am."

"As an NCO, you need to look out for *all* your troops, not only the women." Jackie didn't take the ice out of her voice.

"Yes, ma'am." Green hurried away.

Jackie checked her notes again. She had a few more appointments. Her caffeine intake by this point was probably not making her any easier to talk to. She'd get decaf for the next round.

She had just enough time to use the restroom and refill her cup before the group executive officer arrived.

"Captain Hughes, thanks for meeting me." Jackie stood and shook his hand.

"No worries. Thanks for agreeing to meet here. It'll save me some time. I need to pick up some things for my wife from the Exchange."

They took their seats.

"I know what you're going to ask me," Hughes began. "I encouraged Sergeant Davies to file the complaint."

"You did? He didn't mention that."

"He's protecting me and my job. I know it's hard to prove, but I see it happening again and again. Ms. Shelton prefers men over women—for anything. She treats the women in the office like crap but is sweet as syrup to me." He gave an involuntary shudder.

"Did you ever mention it to her?"

"Not to her, but I did bring it up with the group commander."

"What did he do?"

"He said he'd talk to her but I never saw any change. Wait, I take that back. She was cold to me for a few days after, but then everything was back to normal."

"Did you ever follow up with him?"

"I did. Basically, he told me that she has friends in high places and that trying to do anything to a civilian in the military is too much paperwork."

Jackie's jaw fell open. "Are you kidding me?"

"Nope. His approach was that she wasn't really hurting anything anyway, so it didn't matter."

She shook her head. "That's disgusting."

Hughes passed her a thumb drive. "I've kind of been keeping track of things that might be helpful."

"Did you start this after Sergeant Davies came to you?"

"No, a few months before. That's when I talked to the group commander. I figured if he wasn't going to take me seriously, I needed some ammunition. I jotted down things like work trips and traveling companions. Also award winners."

"Is Ms. Shelton in charge of group awards?" Jackie was dismayed to think how unfair that would be.

"Not really. It's her program but the first sergeant and squadron commanders are the ones who review the nominations and select the winners. She just signs off on them."

"Are the numbers skewed toward men?"

"I don't think so. There are more men than women in the group, so you'll see proportionately more men who win, but I don't think that's her doing."

"Small favors, I guess," Jackie murmured under her breath.

"But there are a couple of other areas where things don't look quite right."

"It was smart to make a record. I really appreciate this."

"Of course. I just hope there's something on there you can use. If you don't mind, I really need to run. You have my cell number. You can call me if you have any questions. Probably not at work. It would be hard to talk freely." He stood.

Jackie stood with him. "It was great meeting you."

After he left, Jackie packed up her notes, dropped her empty cup into the trash, and went back to the chapel. Her next appointment was in thirty minutes in the spare office, and she might have time to look through the notes for a little while before he showed up.

She was transcribing her handwritten notes into the computer when a knock at the door signaled the first sergeant's arrival. She cleared the computer screen before calling for him to enter.

A handsome man in his late thirties, he was polished and respectful as he entered and took the proffered seat.

Jackie was hesitant to ask direct questions, not knowing if Master Sergeant Rhodes was taking advantage of Ms. Shelton's favors as part of his position.

She started her questions generically. "How long have you been the first sergeant for the group?"

"Only about a month. I transferred in from Lackland Air Force Base in Texas."

"Who hired you?" she asked blandly, trying not to let accusation creep into her voice.

"My first interview was with Ms. Shelton, but I work for the group commander directly, so he did the hiring."

She jotted it down. Before she had a chance to ask another question, Master Sergeant Rhodes said, "Can I ask what you're getting at?"

Jackie put on an innocent face. "What do you mean?"

"If you're trying to get to the bottom of the Davies's report, I'm all for it. The accusation hanging out there is killing morale in the group, especially in Davies's squadron."

Jackie relaxed. "Tell me what you think."

"I don't have an opinion yet. I don't know all the players. I've been asking some questions myself and can pass some names on to you. I suggest you talk to them if you haven't already."

"That would be helpful."

"Ms. Shelton is a bit quirky, but everybody is somehow. Definitely too free with her hands. I'm not sure how much she does intentionally and how much is subconscious."

"That's an interesting take," Jackie noted. "Has she tried anything with you?"

His look said it all. "I never get that close to her. This isn't my first rodeo."

Jackie cracked a smile at him.

"I'm pretty disgusted that the SARC took her good old time filing the report to make it official. Davies has been put through the ringer with his peers. Until something is decided one way or the other, he's not going to be able to get past this."

"Why do you think it took so long for the report?"

"If I had to guess, I'd say self-preservation. Lieutenant O'Connor knows Ms. Shelton has pull. Hell, that's one of the first things I found out when I arrived on base. Ms. Shelton knows where the skeletons are buried. As a civilian, she bides her time staying in place as the continuity while military leaders come and go. She knows the local community leaders, the congressmen and women, and the police officials."

He ran his hand through his close-cropped hair. "If you don't mind me saying, that's the price we pay for making civilians such a key part of the Air Force. We've handed over power to people who are hard to discipline or remove when need be. Give me a military leader any day. At least the chain of command is more black and white."

Jackie couldn't argue with that. She had met some incredible government civilians but had also run into the situation where not-so-good workers were moved from place to place without anyone doing the paperwork to kick them out. No one wanted to take on the unions, and military people tended to rotate out of assignments before all the necessary paperwork was completed.

"Do you think Ms. Shelton needs to be replaced?"

"I'm not saying that. I haven't been here long enough to make that kind of judgement."

"You have the ear of the group commander. Has he brought up any concerns?"

"Well, if he did, that would be between us. But I can tell you, he's retiring soon. Any move he made against a civilian could trigger an IG complaint and put a hold on his retirement. Not sure he'd be willing to risk that."

"Ouch."

Master Sergeant Rhodes smiled. "That's one way to put it." He handed her the folded piece of paper he'd been holding. "Here's that list of names. Not sure how many of them Colonel Cheng has already interviewed."

Jackie glanced at the list. "He was mostly concerned with the SARC office audit. He didn't conduct many interviews."

"So you know, the word is out that you're here and asking questions. Mostly people are just curious. Some are starting to wonder if Davies might actually have a legitimate complaint. That's good for him, so thanks for caring."

She gave a wan smile. "I'm sorry it took so long."

"That's how it always works with these things. But it's always better late than never."

Chapter 25

"Everything was wonderful, Carole. Thanks again for having me over." Jackie wiped her mouth and placed her napkin back on her lap. She looked around the dining room, recognizing some of the artwork that had hung in their last house. The wood-carved cross Jackie had sent them from Germany was affixed in a place of honor on the wall leading into the kitchen.

"Let me get you some pie." Carole started to stand, but Jackie halted her with a hand on her arm.

"Please, relax. I couldn't eat another bite."

"She worries about you." The chaplain took his wife's hand.

"I know you work too hard. You always have. And I'm afraid it may have gotten worse—" Carole's sentence went unfinished.

A lump caught in Jackie's throat. "It's been three years. I admit that I threw myself into work at first, but I'm getting better. The move to DC was a fresh start." Not that Jackie felt as whole as she tried to portray. Some things she couldn't outrun, no matter how hard she tried.

"What are you doing outside the office?" Chaplain Vandesteeg asked.

"I ride my bike every day. If the weather's bad, I go to the gym in my apartment complex."

"Those sound like solitary activities. What are you doing to make friends?" he asked.

"Are you dating yet?" Carole tagged on.

Jackie and Vandesteeg turned questioning looks her way.

She waved them off. "Oh, come on. I'm not the only one who wanted to know."

"Well, I would have thought you could have come up with a smoother way to ask," he said.

Jackie laughed. "I've gone out with groups of friends once in a while. Being at the Pentagon isn't the same as being overseas. They don't have squadrons who hang out together."

"But no one has caught your eye?"

Vandesteeg moved his hand to his wife's shoulder to quiet her.

Jackie smoothed the napkin carefully, avoiding their eyes. "I have to admit, I'm starting to notice guys more than I used to." She cleared her throat. "I feel a little guilty about it."

"That's perfectly natural," Vandesteeg said. "For both of those things. It's about time you open yourself up to the idea of dating again. You are so young. And it's only natural to feel a little guilty. You were committed to Stan. But the marriage vows say 'til death do us part.' It's okay to let go now."

Jackie blew out the breath she didn't realize she was holding. She felt a little lighter, as if she had received the permission she was looking for.

After helping do the dinner dishes and dutifully looking at recent family photos, Jackie stifled a yawn. "I want to start early tomorrow so I can leave sooner for home."

"I hope you're getting everything you need here," Vandesteeg said.

"People are helping more than I expected. I'm glad you got me involved."

Carole wrapped her arms around Jackie in a motherly embrace, and Jackie let herself absorb the warmth and love the woman projected. Jackie envied the relationship the chaplain and Carole modeled. She had set them on a pedestal and always wished her marriage was more like theirs. Maybe it was too much; her marriage had been nothing like her expectations.

First Stan's cheating, then the lying. His death had left her wondering if they could have ever fixed it, or if they were doomed from the start.

Now she was widowed at thirty-six, thinking about starting over to see if she had a chance at another relationship.

"Thanks again for everything." She gave the chaplain a quick hug. "See you in the morning."

Jackie reviewed the details of Davies's case in her head as she drove back to the base. Master Sergeant Rhodes was a great first sergeant and very supportive.

A light bulb went on for Jackie, and she made the leap to the Andrews Air Force Base case. She needed to make another appointment with Webster's first sergeant. When she had talked to him before, he was more interested in talking about his commander. Rhodes's mission was to take care of the troops.

The flashing lights in her rearview mirror caught Jackie off guard. She put on her turn signal and quickly pulled to the side of the road to get out of the way.

When the lights pulled in behind her, she rolled down her window and waited while the police officer took his time to approach. All the while, she tried to puzzle out what law she had broken.

Finally, the policeman approached her driver's window, staying slightly behind so Jackie had to turn in her seat to see him. "Do you know how fast you were going?"

"I was going forty-five." She struggled to keep her voice nonconfrontational.

"I clocked you at fifty-four in a forty-five zone."

"That can't be right. I had my cruise control set."

"Well, you obviously had it set too high. You better get that checked. License and registration please."

She handed him the documents.

He walked back to his cruiser as she stewed.

When he returned, he ripped a piece of paper from his ticket book and handed it to her. "I'm letting you go with a warning this time. Have a safe trip home."

Jackie bit her tongue as he walked away. She was careful to use her turn signal as she eased back into traffic and continued on her way.

The cruiser pulled out behind her and stayed on her tail all the way to the McGuire Air Force Base gate. As she turned in, it sped off.

Chapter 26

Jackie finished her interviews the next morning and was typing up her notes when Chaplain Vandesteeg entered. "Haven't seen you all morning. Everything okay?"

She stood and stretched. "I tried to talk to as many people as I could from Master Sergeant Rhodes's list. He's taking this very seriously. Davies is lucky to have him for support."

"Did you learn anything new?"

"Davies was certainly not the only one who found Ms. Shelton to be a little forward in her approach to certain men."

Vandesteeg raised his eyebrows.

"I know. A man would never be considered 'a little forward' in his approach." Jackie made the air quotes. "People would call it what it is—harassment. But no one put it that bluntly to me."

"There's never an excuse when it comes to people in authority. The military takes fraternization very seriously. It should be so much worse when one person is an unwilling participant."

"I agree. So far, I've heard a lot of rumors and gossip, but no one admits having been in a similar situation as Sergeant Davies with Ms. Shelton. I still have a few names to explore who have already left the base."

"Separated or permanent change of station?" Vandesteeg asked.

Jackie glanced at the notes on her desk. "A few of each. But that's a problem for tomorrow. I need to get going. I have a few stops I'd like to make before heading back, and we have soccer practice tonight."

"Traffic shouldn't be too bad today. You're going against the flow."

"I know, but it'll be just my luck that today will be a day when tourists want to head to DC."

Chaplain Vandesteeg held out his arms for a hug. "It was great getting to see you again. Carole loved getting to catch up. Don't make it so long next time."

She gave him a tight squeeze. "Send me a save-the-date for your retirement. I want to make sure I'm off."

"Will do." He left her to finish packing up.

Jackie closed her computer and placed her handwritten notes into the case. She had more questions than answers right now but felt confident she was making progress.

Had other men harassed by Ms. Shelton sought counsel? The SARC was no help. Where would they turn?

Would women support a man who stood up against a female aggressor? Would another man? The question was bigger than this one case.

What she couldn't put her finger on was the reluctance of men to come forward. Was the stigma for them worse than it was for women?

Jackie checked the time. She hoped her drive-bys wouldn't take too long. She entered the first address into the GPS and followed the directions to her first stop.

Pulling into one of the many empty parking spots in front of the office building, Jackie took a picture of the for sale sign with her cell phone. At the next address, the picture windows were covered from the inside, and a large sign provided the number to call for a great deal on renting this space. Jackie snapped a photo of it as well, then looked around at the many empty storefronts lining this section of town.

Her last stop was on the way to the highway. At one time, it had been the home of a fast-food chain restaurant. From the weeds breaking through the cracks in the parking lot, Jackie assumed it had been out of business a long time. The realtor's sign sported graffiti that covered any contact information. She took the picture anyway and pointed her car toward the entrance ramp.

~

"I'm so glad you're back." Leon wrapped his arms around Jackie in an exaggerated hug born of desperation.

She laughed. "It couldn't have been that bad."

"Are you kidding? I was almost overrun. Thankfully, some of the parents stepped up to help. These kids can be vicious."

"It was only one practice, but it's nice to be appreciated."

Jackie set up the orange cones for the drills as the first few kids arrived.

"How was your trip? Did you get the answers you were looking for?" Leon asked.

"Yes and no. The Air Force has a long way to go before people get what they deserve—both good and bad. I got to catch up with old friends, though."

Leon hefted the water jug onto the bench. "How are things with your investigation at Andrews? Is that Webster character giving you any trouble?"

"I've been laying low there, trying to stay on my boss's good side. I'm setting up a meeting with Master Sergeant Preston tomorrow. I'm hoping, as the first sergeant, he can give me more insight into this situation."

"Good idea. The shirt usually knows all the scuttlebutt in the squadron." Leon dumped the soccer balls out of the bag.

"Davies's first sergeant at McGuire was very involved. It got me thinking that I didn't spend enough time talking to Preston."

Little arms wrapping around her legs threw Jackie off balance. She laughed and hugged the petite girl.

"Hey, Kendra. Ready to play soccer?"

"Can we play tag instead?"

Jackie smiled. "Go play for a few minutes while we wait for the others."

Kendra spun in circles as she made her way to the cluster of children already on the field.

"That kid has really taken a liking to you," Leon said.

"She's sweet. And not a bad player for her age."

"Her dad practices with her at home."

"It shows. He must know what he's doing."

The parents gathered on the benches in the shade to wait out the practice while Leon blew his whistle to gather the kids around him.

Jackie joined them as they jogged around the field singing the songs Leon created.

While they were lining up near the goal line, Jackie gazed around the park. The swing sets were full, as were the benches where the parents waited for their children to run out of energy.

A chill ran down Jackie's spine, and she tried to shrug it off. She looked deeper into the shadows under the trees, trying to discover the cause of her discomfort. Was someone leaning against the trunk? Jackie strained her eyes but couldn't make out the figure. Maybe it was her imagination.

Leon's whistle rang out sharply. Jackie got back to work, leading the young players through a set of drills neatly disguised as a fun-filled game.

The shadow in the trees was forgotten.

Chapter 27

While Jackie waited in her loaner office at Andrews Air Force Base for Master Sergeant Preston to arrive, she reviewed her notes from the first time they talked. He hadn't offered anything important. Where Sergeant Reynolds had immediately started looking into the welfare of the troops, Preston concentrated on defending his commander.

"Ma'am, you asked to see me?"

"Please come in." She walked around the desk and took a seat in an adjacent chair so she there was no barrier between them.

"I had a few follow-up questions for you. Let's talk about Senior Airman Amanda Nelson."

"Anything I can do to help. I feel bad for her."

"She's going through a lot right now. I understand some members of the squadron are giving her a hard time."

"It's to be expected." He crossed his legs, resting his elbows on the arms of the chair. "No one wants to be the snitch, but you can't let people get away with this kind of behavior. It's not good for morale."

"Or the person being attacked."

"Well, that goes without saying." Something about his sideways smirk raised the hair on the back of Jackie's neck.

"During our first chat, you mentioned the victims were

getting the help they needed. I assume you are checking in on them from time to time. How's Airman Nelson doing now?"

"Getting stronger every day. She'll be better when this is all behind her."

"Is it true she has requested a transfer?"

"That's perfectly normal in her situation. There's a stink with this kind of case. Victims want to distance themselves from it."

"You sound like you've dealt with this situation before."

"We talked about it at first sergeant school, of course. Sadly, it isn't uncommon. Amanda is lucky she has a supportive boss like Colonel Webster to look out for her."

"Interesting that you should say that. She doesn't feel that lucky."

He tilted his head questioningly.

She went on. "Airman Nelson says she never reported a rape to Colonel Webster."

Preston scratched behind his ear. "I believe it came in from a third party."

"Who made the report?"

"That's confidential."

"This is an unrestricted report. Nothing is confidential about it."

"If people don't feel comfortable taking matters to the commander in confidence, they will stop coming to him. We can't let that happen."

She crossed her hands over her notes. "So tell me, how did you hear about Airman Nelson's alleged rape?"

"Rape is rape. There's no *alleged* about it."

Jackie waited in silence for him to go on.

When she didn't rise to his bait, he said, "Someone close to Amanda came forward because she was concerned about Amanda's state of mind after the incident."

"Who was this person?"

"She wants to remain anonymous. Respecting that is the only way this system works. If people can't trust their first shirt to keep a secret, who can they trust?"

"I spoke with Airman Suzanne Zala. She says she confided in you when you kept pestering her about something being wrong with Airman Nelson."

"Yes. I do remember having a talk with her about that. She was deeply concerned for Amanda's well-being."

"That's not how she tells it. She says she told you Airman Nelson was fine; she was just having men-problems."

"That's what she said at first. But the more we talked, she opened up. She mentioned Amanda spending the night in Mac's room."

"And you heard that and jumped to rape?"

"That airman is young and impressionable. A staff sergeant should not have taken advantage of her. He knows better."

"What if she took advantage of him?"

Preston reacted as if he had been slapped. "If you are going to make light of this, I don't think I'm interested in wasting my time with you."

Jackie cocked an eyebrow.

Clearing his throat, Preston tried to dig himself out of the hole he had fallen into. "I don't mean to be disrespectful, ma'am. I'm just concerned you aren't taking this seriously."

"I'm taking this very seriously. Along with all the other cases that cross my desk."

"Does it really matter how I found out? The important thing is that Amanda gets the help she needs."

Jackie let that go. "What was Airman Nelson's state of mind when you talked to her?"

"She was distraught. Afraid her boyfriend was going to find out."

"Find out that she slept with someone else?"

"Find out someone had taken advantage of her."

Jackie crossed her legs and took a moment to answer. "Is that what she said?"

"She was so upset when she was in my office, she couldn't string two words together."

"Could her condition have been for a different reason than having been raped? Like embarrassment over talking to her first shirt about sex?"

"I can't believe you—a woman—are doubting the seriousness of this accusation! We can't let this behavior slide even one time."

"I'm not suggesting we let anything slide. I'm trying to get to the bottom of the complaint. Airman Nelson says she wasn't raped. She was upset because she regretted sleeping with Sergeant Morgan, and yes, she didn't want her boyfriend to find out."

Master Sergeant Preston leaned forward. The veins on his forearms were pulsing.

"That's what she says now. She's been under a lot of pressure by Mac's friends, so she's changing her story. That's the danger of letting these things drag on too long. Amanda's confused."

"But, for the sake of argument, let's say she wasn't raped. That she was a willing participant, as she claims. Couldn't it also be true she was upset because she felt like she had cheated on her boyfriend, and she didn't want him to know? Wouldn't that explain her mood when you called her into your office?"

"You haven't seen as many cases as I have, colonel. I can tell when someone has been assaulted."

Jackie let that hang in the air. After several seconds, she stood. "Thank you for coming in. I appreciate all you're doing to help the victims in your unit." She offered her hand.

He stood and shook it. A little wind had left his sails.

"Thank you for being so thorough in your follow-up. These women deserve someone in the Pentagon looking out for them."

As she left the office, Jackie spotted Colonel Dellinger in the hall talking to the operations group commander. Smoothing her hair to catch any stray strands, she straightened her back and tried to be casual as she walked his way.

When she was only steps away, the men shook hands, and the group commander departed. Colonel Dellinger caught her eye.

"Jackie, nice to see you. Are you getting everything you need for your investigation?"

"Yes, sir. Thank you. I appreciate the use of the spare office. It's a lot easier than having to find a different place every time I need to talk to someone."

"Glad we had a place for you. The office will be filled next month."

They stood awkwardly, nothing else to say.

"I better—"

"Well—"

They spoke at once. Then they laughed.

"It was nice seeing you again. Let me know if there's anything else I can do."

"Thank you. I will." She watched as he walked back to his office. When he glanced over his shoulder, she hurried out the front door of the building.

"What's up? You sounded pissed." Leon slid into a seat across the table from Jackie. True friend that he was, he'd come to their usual spot in the food court as soon as she called. He didn't even stop for coffee.

"I want to hit something." Jackie spoke through gritted teeth.

"Or someone?"

"Ugh! Preston has such a cocky attitude!"

"Oh, you met with the first sergeant. It didn't go well, I take it."

"He and Webster are drinking the same Kool-Aid."

"What do you mean?"

Jackie peeled the label from the bottle of water she was fidgeting with. "Webster is so sure he's helping the women in his squadron, and Preston's spouting the same crap. They aren't listening! They're doing more harm than good."

"I know one of the women has talked to you. Have you tried talking to any of the others?"

"Yeah, and they say about the same thing. They didn't make the complaint; they just got dragged into it."

"What about the accused?"

"What about them? In most cases, the charges were dropped."

"But were they dropped because the OSI didn't have enough info or because the men were innocent?"

Jackie tilted her head. "What are you getting at?"

"Think of how their lives were altered if they were falsely accused. It's much harder for men to internalize the need to support women who may have been assaulted when, at any moment, they know their lives can be upturned because of a misrepresentation or misunderstanding. Or a vengeful spirit."

"Don't tell me you are seriously buying into the men-are-being-persecuted bull."

Leon put a hand on Jackie's arm to calm her down. "I'm not saying that. We need to take out the bad guys. That's what we do. We just have to be careful not to take out innocents in the frag pattern. Look at the situation with Davies. Many people assume your office was set up to protect women. But it's not. It's to protect the victim."

He had her full attention. "Now that you are helping the victims, what are you doing to help the wrongly accused? They're victims too. You have to look at the problem from both sides."

Chapter 28

The next morning found Jackie on her way back to the Hill. She didn't realize how political this job would be when she volunteered for the assignment.

She used her time on the shuttle to answer emails on her phone and check her calendar for the next few days. Another trip to the Hill meant rearranging her whole afternoon.

When she finished, she stuffed her phone into her bag. "This Kirkson guy is a piece of work."

From his seat behind her, Major Wilson watched the scenery as the bus lumbered through the traffic. "I think his parents are worse. He didn't get like that on his own."

"Last week, I went to McGuire to meet with Sergeant Davies. Afterward, I drove by a few of the Kirkson properties. I don't think they are doing as well as the congressman thinks they are."

"Why do you say that?" Wilson asked.

"All three of the places I drove by were for sale. They own more but I didn't have time to hit them all."

"Do you have a list?"

She raised an eyebrow at him. "I do. Why?"

"I can do a little snooping for you. I know my way around the legal-eeze of state and county records."

"Is this part of your job or a side hobby?"

"Let's just say I've done my share of research projects in the past." A small smile appeared briefly, then was gone. That was the most Jackie had ever seen of the major's emotions.

A loud squeal of brakes, followed by the hiss of air escaping indicated it was their stop.

Jackie allowed Major Wilson to lead her through the corridors of the Cannon House office building again. She had no expectations this time of getting out at a reasonable hour so was surprised when Charlie showed up and escorted them into a conference room only an hour after their scheduled meeting time.

"Sorry I missed you last time," the staffer said. "You know how things go. We're at the whim of the machine."

Jackie bit back her retort.

She noticed he was still in need of a shave, but at least his shirt was tucked in this time. The dark circles under his eyes were pronounced against his pale skin.

"You have an update for me on Airman Kirkson?"

"He's a staff sergeant," Jackie corrected. "Is the congressman aware Sergeant Kirkson has been picked up multiple times for driving under the influence?"

"No. Should he be?"

Jackie cleared her throat and tried to control her impatience. "It's my understanding from the investigators on the case that Sergeant Kirkson was picked up but never charged because someone got involved and made the charges go away."

"If the charges went away, as you say, how do you know about them?"

"Our investigators are diligent. They don't just sift through papers."

Charlie looked at her with a blank expression.

"They asked around."

"So it's rumors. That's all you've got?" Charlie stood.

"I thought the congressman would like to know, since he is so invested in Kirkson's case."

"I'll let him know."

"How about I just email you with updates from now on?" Jackie asked.

"I don't mind the face-to-face meetings," he said. "Emails feel so impersonal."

He was out the door before Jackie could think of a polite comeback.

"Nice try," Major Wilson said.

Chapter 29

The wind whistled through her helmet as Jackie raced along the bike path. It had been a frustrating week, and she needed to take it out on her muscles. Sweat rolled down her back, pooling into an uncomfortable wet spot at her waistband.

It was early Sunday morning, and Jackie hadn't seen anyone on the path. Very few cars were out, and the temperature was perfect. A few red leaves dotted the green trees. It was a great fall day.

As she entered a neighborhood, the bike path transitioned from a raised area next to the sidewalk to an extra lane on the road. Jackie shifted gears to keep her feet moving but slowed her pace.

Unbidden, thoughts of what Master Sergeant Preston said to her flooded her mind.

Did he really think he was helping those women? If he was the problem, did Webster know what was going on or was he oblivious?

Jackie wanted to talk to Webster again. This time she would do it right. She needed to talk to her boss, then let Colonel Dellinger know. At that thought, she felt a tingle of excitement. She chided herself for thinking of him that way.

A flash of metal caught her eye. She turned her head to get a better look. Before her mind registered the mass racing toward her, she was catapulted through the air. The loud snap of bone took her breath away, and she landed in a heap, tangled in the bike.

Screeching tires and the whir of her upturned wheels spinning filled her ears before things went black.

～

"Ma'am, can you hear me? Can you hear me?"

Jackie tried to turn her head toward the voice and caught the flashing lights through her eyelids. She wanted to open her eyes, but it hurt too much.

"Don't move. I'm going to put this collar on you. You're going to be fine. We're going to take you to the hospital to get checked out."

"Bike," Jackie mumbled.

The EMT chuckled. "Probably time to upgrade anyway."

They moved Jackie to a backboard and lifted her quickly. The world tilted for a moment, and she thought she was going to be sick.

"Hang in there," the EMT said.

Jackie slowly opened her eyes and took it all in as the doors slammed shut and the ambulance pulled out. The two people with her were efficient, as if they had been working together for years.

"It's a short ride. We'll be there in no time," one said to her as she took Jackie's blood pressure. "One thirty over ninety-five."

The other scribbled something on a tablet.

True to their word, the ride was short and soon Jackie was being wheeled into the emergency room.

"Hit and run. Victim was riding a bike. BP one-thirty over ninety-five. Arm splinted at the scene."

"Can you tell me your name?"

It took a second for Jackie to realize the person was talking to her. "Jackie Austin."

The woman shined a penlight into Jackie's left, then right eye. "Jackie, I'm Doctor Evans. Do you remember what happened?"

Her mouth was dry, and it was hard to speak. She croaked out, "I was riding my bike."

"Did you see the car hit you?"

"What car?"

"I'll take that as a no." The doctor turned to a person waiting nearby. "Get a head CT and an x-ray on her arm."

Turning back to Jackie, she asked, "Does your neck hurt?"

"No."

"What about anywhere else?"

Jackie thought about it. Besides the throbbing of her left arm, she just felt sore. "My arm."

"That's to be expected. It didn't break the skin, but your arm is obviously broken. We'll set it after we see the x-ray. Let's get this helmet off."

The doctor unclipped the strap and gently lifted it from her head. Then she released the collar around her neck. Running her fingers over Jackie's scalp, she gave a curt nod. "The helmet did its job. Your head's in one piece, but you're going to have quite a headache."

"Already do," Jackie said.

"Are you allergic to anything?"

"No."

"Let's get her something for the pain." She pushed and prodded at Jackie's abdomen and ran her hands down Jackie's legs. "Wiggle your toes. Does it hurt?"

Jackie did as she was told. "No."

"Is there someone we can call for you while you wait for your tests?"

She certainly didn't want to call her mother. "Is my phone here?"

"I don't see it, but we'll check with the EMTs."

"Can you call my boss?" Jackie didn't know the number from memory but told the doctor where she worked and gave her Major General Varn's name.

The nurse standing in the doorway nodded. "Got it. I'll track her down."

The doctor patted her shoulder. "I'll be back with you after your scans."

Jackie closed her eyes. She really wanted to sleep.

Chapter 30

When Jackie awoke, her boss was at her bedside. In jeans and an old sweatshirt, Jackie hardly recognized her. "Sorry to call you on a Sunday."

"You would have been in big trouble if you hadn't," Varn said, but her voice was soft and kind. "How are you feeling?"

"Been better."

"Let me get the doctor. She came by while you were sleeping."

Major General Varn slipped out through the curtain.

Jackie's head was swimming. The last thing she remembered was that she needed an x-ray.

Doctor Evans came back, followed by the general.

"Your forearm is fractured in two places. You're lucky it's still aligned. It'll heal in about twelve weeks but no bike riding in the meantime, and I don't want you lifting with that arm until you get into physical therapy. You have a concussion, so we're going to keep you at least overnight and watch you."

For the first time, Jackie noticed the ice pack around her left forearm. "Can I sit up?"

"Sure." Doctor Evans pushed the button to raise the head of the bed. "Do you need anything else?"

"Water."

"I'll get it," her boss said.

"I'll be back later." The doctor dashed off to her next patient.

Varn held a cup with water and straw. "Just a little."

"What time is it?"

"Almost four o'clock."

"What the–"

"Don't worry about it. You've got nowhere to be more important than this."

Jackie closed her eyes again. How could she still be so tired?

"I'll let you rest. Do you want me to call your parents?"

Her eyes snapped open. "No!"

"Relax. I won't unless you want me to."

Just as she was dozing off, a gruff voice interrupted her. "Miss Austin?"

"Lieutenant Colonel Austin," she responded automatically.

"Lieutenant Colonel Austin, I apologize. I have a few questions for you if you feel up to it." A young police officer dressed in a light blue shirt and dark pants stood in the doorway. A radio attached to his shoulder crackled.

She waved him in.

"Did you see the car that hit you?"

Jackie replayed what happened in her mind's eye. "Not really. It came from behind on my left side. I saw something shiny just before I was hit. There were no cars in front of me."

"A person living nearby heard the car speeding away and looked out his window. He's the one who called the ambulance."

"I need his name to send a thank you note."

"It'll be in the report. Is there any reason to think this was anything more than a random hit and run?"

She shook her head and instantly regretted it. Her head was still pounding.

"Okay. If you think of anything else, please give me a call." He handed her a card.

When he left the room, Major General Varn followed him. Whispers filtered through the curtains, but Jackie couldn't make them out. She drifted off to sleep.

When she opened her eyes again, it wasn't so painful. The lights were low, and her head felt as if the stabbing needles had been removed.

A shuffle in the corner drew her attention. A human shape was outlined by the faint light coming through the drawn curtains. Jackie's first thought was of the stalker who had attacked her in her home. She fought for control of her heart as she remembered she was in a hospital. She was safe here.

"Hello?" she said tentatively.

The shape leaned forward in the chair. "Sorry, I didn't mean to wake you."

"Colonel Dellinger?"

He stood and approached the bed. "When you missed our meeting today, I was worried. It's not like you."

"It's Monday already? I'm sorry. I didn't realize."

"You had a few other things on your mind. General Varn was just here. She went down to get some coffee. I told her I'd sit with you until she got back."

Jackie tried to push herself up on the mattress.

"Here. Let me help." He handed her the remote for her bed, then held onto the pillow as she got comfortable.

She was self-conscious having him so close. Her hair was probably a mess. She automatically reached up to smooth it down and was unprepared for the weight of the cast and the cumbersome sling. Her left arm stopped awkwardly before reaching her head. She let it fall back.

Trying her best to sound natural, she said, "You didn't need to come all the way down here."

He gave a one shoulder shrug. "It's on the base. Nothing's that far."

"Good point." *What a stupid thing to say. Of course he didn't go out of his way for me.*

"Wait? I'm on base?"

"The EMTs saw your military ID so they brought you here. You weren't in immediate danger."

"Oh." Jackie couldn't think of anything else to say. She wasn't sure if her brain was fuzzy from the concussion or the pain medication.

"I was on my way to lunch when General Varn called to let me know what happened. I thought I'd swing by and see if there was anything I could do for you."

A flush rose to her cheeks at the thought of him doing something for her. *Probably not what he meant.*

"That's very nice of you, sir. They should let me go home today."

"Maybe I can check up on you later in the week. Make sure you're healing."

His smile was soft, and Jackie caught herself staring at his lips. "That would be nice, but I know you're busy."

"Not too busy."

She tried to think of a response that wouldn't sound stupid.

"Wonderful! You're awake." Varn's voice interrupted the awkward silence that had fallen between Jackie and the wing commander.

"I should get going." Colonel Dellinger moved toward the door. "We'll reschedule our meeting when you're feeling up to it," he told Jackie. "No rush."

"Thanks for coming, sir," she called after him.

Varn stood beside Jackie's bed. "How are you feeling?"

"Tired."

"To be expected. Are you up for one more visitor? There's a major waiting to see you."

"Sure."

"Then I'm going to get back to work and let you visit. I just wanted to make sure you were okay."

"I'll be fine, ma'am. Thanks for everything."

Varn smiled. "Take it easy. Let me know if you need a ride home."

When Varn left, Leon slipped through the door carrying a bouquet. "I didn't even rate a phone call? I thought we were friends."

She grinned at him. "Of course we are. How'd you find out where I was?"

"I stopped by your cubicle so you could buy me coffee this morning, and Sergeant Polk filled me in. Are you okay?"

"I will be, although this cast is going to slow me down on the soccer field."

"You were pretty slow to begin with."

Jackie punched his shoulder. "I could leave you to coach all alone."

"Let's not be so hasty. The fresh air will probably do you good." His face turned serious. "What happened?"

"Hit and run while I was riding my bike. The cops took a statement, but I'm not holding my breath."

"Is there anything I can do? Besides lend you my bike. That's not happening."

"Check with the nurse to see if I can get out of here, will you? Then you can take me home."

Chapter 31

"Why are you back at work?" Varn asked.

Jackie shrugged. "I can't sit around at home. I'm going stir-crazy. It's been a week."

Varn leaned over her desk to examine Jackie as if she were x-raying her wounds and assessing her healing properties. "You need to take it easy."

"I will, but I'd like your permission to talk to Colonel Webster again."

"That's your idea of taking it easy?" She frowned.

"Talking isn't very strenuous." Jackie tried to come across as light-hearted. She really wanted to get to the bottom of whatever was going on in Webster's squadron. It was eating away at her.

"Do you have new information?" Varn asked.

"No, I just want to ask a few follow-up questions." Jackie had stayed home as long as she could but was itching to finish what she had started. Something about the way Webster treated women rubbed her the wrong way. He wasn't cruel; actually, he was almost too . . . solicitous.

"What does Colonel Dellinger say?"

"I wanted to ask you first."

"Can you keep your cool?"

Jackie looked shamefaced; she had been corrected for her quick tongue before. "Yes, ma'am."

"Tread carefully. It might help to have somebody else with you when you meet. What about Colonel Cheng?"

"Actually, I'd like to send Cheng back to McGuire. The commander agreed to have the SARC removed, so I'd like him to step in and facilitate the transition and do a little more digging." Inwardly, Jackie prayed her boss would go along with this plan. It was a great opportunity to get Cheng more visibility before his next promotion board.

"Do we have the man-days for that?"

"Yes, ma'am. And I can request additional if it looks like it'll take more than a week or two."

"Go ahead. But find someone else to go with you to see Webster. It'd be safer if you weren't driving one-handed anyway."

Major General Varn shifted gears. "What about Wright-Pat?"

Jackie rolled her eyes. "It doesn't look like the director is taking it seriously. From what I hear, OSI has turned over their findings to the judge advocate, but the director is ignoring their advice. I can't say that officially, of course."

"Have you talked to the young lady's counsel?"

"Yes, ma'am. The victim is most certainly willing to go to trial if need be."

"Then sounds like we have some work to do. Have you talked to the director?"

"No, ma'am. I thought I'd leave that up to you."

Varn gave her a suspicious look, but Jackie ignored it. She was trying her best to learn from past mistakes and wasn't about to get snapped at again for overreaching.

"Let me ask around about the players. There are almost as many civilians as military at Wright-Pat, and they tend to stick around longer."

"Is that a good thing or a bad thing?" Jackie had her own opinion but wanted to see where her boss stood on the subject.

"Can be both. Continuity is helpful when the military personnel move every few years."

"But?" Jackie nudged when Varn didn't finish her thought.

Varn took her time answering, studying Jackie before deciding on her words. "But it can be hard to move forward with new ideas when folks get set in their ways. They get too comfortable at times."

"And they don't want to rock the boat they're sitting in?"

"Exactly."

~

Jackie was waiting in Dellinger's outer office when he came through the doors. He stopped short when he saw her.

"Jackie, how are you feeling?"

"Good enough to get back to work."

"You got your hair cut. It looks nice."

She lifted her casted arm, still in a sling. "Kind of tough to put up my hair one handed."

He brushed the short hair by his ear. "Don't I know it."

They exchanged a smile.

"What brings you in?" he asked.

"I wanted to visit Colonel Webster again."

"Are you sure you're up for it? Should you even be back at work?"

"I feel fine." She indicated her cast. "Except for this, of course. But that won't affect how I ask questions."

She gestured to Renko. "This is Sergeant Renko. He works in our analysis section. He's going to be with me."

The men shook hands.

"You have my blessing to talk to him. Just tread lightly. He's very sensitive on this issue," Dellinger said.

"Sir, I will be very careful. That's the real reason General Varn sent Sergeant Renko along. To keep me out of trouble."

Dellinger looked Renko in the eye. "Good luck, sergeant. You'll need it."

"Jackie, you look awful." Webster met her with an outstretched hand. Seeing her left arm in a sling and right hand carrying a notebook, he dropped his hand awkwardly.

Her hackles were up but she wasn't sure if it was because of the insult or the use of her first name without permission. They weren't friends. "Quite the charmer, aren't you?"

"Sorry. I meant no offense. What happened to you?"

"A little run in with a car. Nothing to worry about."

"Are you sure?" Webster leaned into her personal space, examining her face more closely. "Those don't look like the kind of marks you get from a traffic accident."

She stepped back to put more separation between them. "I'm not here to discuss me."

"Well, if you ever need to talk, I've been told I'm a good listener." He repositioned himself behind his desk.

"This is Sergeant Renko from our office."

Webster inclined his head in acknowledgement. "What brings you two in today?"

"I wanted to ask you a few more questions."

"Have a seat."

She took a moment to get organized, juggling the notepad on her lap. "You've had a number of sexual assault and harassment cases in the last six months."

"I already told you, I can't talk to you about those. The final punishments haven't been presented yet in all the cases."

"I'm not looking for details. I'm just wondering how you handle so many cases at once."

"Each one is unique. I look at each one on its own merit."

"But that has to be disconcerting. So many cases of sexual harassment or assault happening right under your nose."

He stiffened.

Renko cleared his throat in warning.

Jackie went on. "Makes me curious about the climate in your unit that so many people think they can get away with treating people like this."

"They aren't getting away with it. I'm investigating each one."

"I pulled the last climate survey for your squadron that was taken just before your predecessor left. Looks like you were handed a squared-away unit." She made a show of looking at her notes. "I noticed you had this problem in your last squadron."

His fingers curled into fists. "I thought you had questions for me. If you aren't going to ask them, I have work to do."

She ignored him. "Your current cases are all unrestricted. Did the women come in on their own or did a friend bring them?"

"What does that matter?"

"I'm trying to get a sense of the camaraderie within your unit. Do the victims feel they have the support from their friends?"

"They have my support. That's enough."

"No, actually, it isn't. We have SARCs in place to ensure the victims get what they need. And, if you've ever talked to a SARC, you'd know having friends to talk to is important for healing."

Webster shrugged off her comment. "I can only control my actions. I obviously can't be their friend, but I am there for them. Whatever they need."

"So back to my question. Did they come in on their own?"

"I'd have to double check. But I would say it was half and half."

Jackie didn't have to look at her notes. "Actually, none of the victims came to you, isn't that right?"

Webster was taken aback. "What do you mean?"

"All six of the alleged victims were brought to your attention through a third-party."

He said nothing.

"That seems like a weird coincidence." She gave him time to respond but he continued his silence.

Renko finally spoke up. "In case you were wondering, that's not typical in other units."

Webster looked as if he had forgotten the sergeant was there.

"What are you accusing me of?"

"Looks to me like you might be shaking the bushes to see what falls out," Jackie said.

Webster stood. "If you don't have any more questions, it's time for me to get back to work."

Jackie and Renko headed for the door. As Renko reached for the handle, Webster said, "I was serious. If you want to talk about what really caused those marks on your face, you can come by any time."

When they were out of the building, Renko rolled his shoulders. "He's creepy."

Jackie released a short laugh. "That's one way to put it."

"What do you think is really going on?"

"I'm not sure yet. But something's not quite right." She shifted the bag on her shoulder.

"What would anyone get from drumming up sexual assault cases?"

"Attention?"

"But that's not the kind of attention most squadrons are looking for. It usually means trouble."

"Covering something up?" Jackie couldn't put her finger on it.

They reached the car, and Renko held the passenger door open for Jackie. "Oh, I have the list of transfers out of Webster's squadron you asked for. I'll send you their current locations as soon as we get back."

Jackie raised one eyebrow. "What took you so long?"

"I've had them. But *someone* was in the hospital, then taking time off. I didn't think it was a priority."

She smiled at his jab.

"Some on the list are at the Pentagon," he said.

"Makes sense. It's a change of station without having to move your household."

"Maybe we should talk to them. They weren't involved in any of the reports from Colonel Webster's units. Perhaps they can give us another perspective. Or there may be no connection at all."

"We? Have I recruited you into one of my pet projects?" Her mouth lifted on one side into a smirk.

"I'm invested now, ma'am. I need to know how it ends."

"I'm glad for the help. Remember, your job is to keep me out of trouble. Go ahead and set it up."

Chapter 32

The first game was underway. Jackie tried to keep the kids from clustering around the ball, calling their names and pointing with her good arm to their correct positions. Leon was bringing kids on and off the field to make sure everyone got playing time and plenty of water.

At halftime, all the kids gathered around the bench to drink and have a piece of watermelon. Looking around for the nearest trash can, Jackie spied Colonel Dellinger walking toward the bleachers. She felt a blush color her face. Then chastised herself because he obviously wasn't there to see her.

He searched the bleachers, then made his way to a seat next to Veronica, who excitedly filled him in on the events of the first half, pointing and laughing.

Jackie's heart dropped. She thought he was single. Never even considered he had a wife and daughter.

Wasn't Veronica Kendra's mother? What were the chances his daughter would be on the team Jackie was helping with?

Just then, Dellinger glanced up and saw Jackie. He waved, a confused look on his face, as if he were wondering the same thing.

The warning whistle sounded. Jackie dumped the watermelon rinds into a trash bin and went back to the team.

She had a hard time focusing on the rest of the game, a little disheartened without wanting to admit why.

At the end of the game, the kids finished up their snacks, and Jackie and Leon cleaned up after them. Parents thanked them as they picked up their charges, heading for home.

"You two do a great job with the kids."

Jackie turned toward the voice, and Colonel Dellinger stood a few feet away, his hands lovingly on Kendra's shoulders.

Leon shook his hand. "We love it. Plus, it's more for us than it is for them. We get to act like kids again."

They laughed. Jackie tried to join in, but there was still a knot in her stomach she couldn't explain.

"You're a woman of many talents," Dellinger said to Jackie. "I didn't know you played soccer."

And I didn't know you had a daughter, she thought. "I don't really. Vicki begged me to help."

He nodded. "Well, we better get going. We promised Kendra ice cream for her goal today."

"Keep up the good work, Kendra. You're doing great," Leon said.

Kendra hugged Jackie and gave Leon a high-five before walking away hand-in-hand with her father.

Leon called Vicki over to help them carry equipment to the truck. "How do you know Kendra's dad?"

"He's the wing commander at Andrews."

"Really? I would never have guessed. He's really down to earth. He's one of the fathers who helped while you were at McGuire. Maybe we should ask him to help more often."

"Let's not."

Leon gave her a funny look.

"I'm sure he's busy. He didn't even make it here until halftime." She concentrated on emptying the water jugs one-handed rather than answering the question on his face.

Chapter 33

"Jackie, this place is more of a mess than we originally thought," Lieutenant Colonel Cheng said over the phone. "After you had O'Connor removed, I had a chance to go through her emails. Good thing you didn't give her enough notice to clean house."

The rain pounded against the window in her cubicle. Jackie subconsciously counted the seconds between the lightning flash and the thunderclap.

"What did you find?" she asked after the rumbling stopped.

"I did a quick search by Shelton's name and hit the lottery. Quite a few tips were emailed to the office. O'Connor responded that she'd look into it, but I didn't see any follow-up reports or cases."

"Interesting. Were they all men?"

"No, actually. But most of the emails from the women were complaints about favoritism toward the men. From the sounds of it, they aren't blaming it on the men. It's all against Shelton. The pattern of favoritism is definitely there."

"How did O'Connor not pick up on this trend?" Jackie was furious.

"Maybe she did, but it benefited her to keep quiet."

"I can't imagine how."

"People say Shelton's connected. Maybe O'Connor was lining up her post-military job."

"She should have been concentrating on doing *this* job. I can't understand how people can be so selfish."

"Agree. I'm going to turn it all over to OSI. It might help them when they start the investigation against Shelton."

The lightning caught her eye again. "What's next?"

"I already followed up with a few of the senders. Some men asked about the process of filing a complaint and who would have to know. Seems they're gun shy because of the treatment Davies is getting."

"Are any of them willing to go on record?"

"Not yet, but I have an idea. I'm thinking if I can get them together in a room, they might support each other and be willing to speak up."

"Great plan. How soon can you set that up?"

"Couple of days. Who's going to notify the wing commander if this is as bad as we think it is?"

"Major General Varn. That's why she's paid the big bucks."

Cheng chuckled softly. "Tell her before I get back in the office, please. I don't want to be in her line of fire."

"Hey, check in on Davies, will you? Let him know you're working something. I don't want him to think we dropped him."

"No problem."

As she hung up, a huge boom rattled the windows.

She drafted a short email to her boss; she had a feeling this was going to get dicey.

Jackie was in her boss's office early the next morning.

"As you can imagine, the McGuire wing commander isn't at all thrilled about the turn of events. He insists Shelton is one of the best group commanders he has ever worked with," Varn said.

"That's not surprising, is it? He's male and a fighter pilot."

"Jackie." Varn's tone put her in her place.

"Sorry, ma'am." As always, she struggled to push down her negative opinions about how the fighter pilots ran the Air Force just because they were good pilots. They didn't necessarily have to be good leaders.

"He's more upset the SARC never brought these concerns to his attention." Varn picked up a pen and clicked it open and closed several times.

"He hadn't heard about Davies?"

"Only when Chaplain Vandesteeg cornered him at an event to discuss it with him, but the chaplain couldn't release any details due to his position. The only real blip on his radar was the police blotter when Sergeant Davies's car was vandalized."

"But the commander is still siding with Shelton over a sexual harassment victim?" Jackie fought to hide the disgust she felt.

"Let's just say he's hoping Shelton isn't guilty."

Jackie thought about what Cheng had said. "Could she have something on him? The wing commander, I mean. During the interviews, everyone talked about her connections."

"I don't think we should look for a conspiracy. The wing commander is doing his job watching out for his people."

Not all his people, Jackie thought.

Chapter 34

Jackie sat behind Major General Varn's desk but off to the side to avoid being on the camera. She had a perfect view of the entire call. Varn was centered on the screen during the video call with Mr. Floyd Chasteen, the director of Erin Mollner's department.

"I'm sorry you were bothered by this, but I've got it under control," the weasel-looking man on the other end was saying.

"The idea someone felt the need to place the call is what has me bothered," Varn answered.

"Well, there was no need for that at all. We have everything under control here."

"It doesn't sound that way. It sounds like the victim's rights to face her attacker has been ignored." Varn's tone remained calm and neutral. Under the desk, her fists clenched and unclenched, but she gave nothing away through the camera.

"It's not like that at all. It's an unfortunate case. Really, if you think about it, this is much better for everyone all the way around." The man shuffled papers on his desk, the sound amplified by the microphone.

Varn stayed silent.

Seeming to be very interested in something on his desk, Chasteen said, "This way, the young lady doesn't have to relive her experience in front of a courtroom full of people."

When Varn still didn't say anything, Chasteen went on nervously. "Imagine how many lives could be ruined by one drunken man's error. Is it really worth it?"

Her steely eyes bore a hole through the miles.

He threw up his hands in surrender. "You know how it is. The congressman called. Asked for a little favor. I figured no one was really hurt, and we might be able to get some help on that initiative we've been trying to push through."

The slow burn Jackie was feeling was reflected on Major General Varn's face.

"Does your boss know about this?" Varn's lips were a pale, thin line.

"He didn't need to get involved. We handled it at the lowest level. It was the best thing for everyone. No sense ruining a young man's career over a stupid mistake."

"And what about the young woman's life?" Varn was barely able to get the words out through her clenched teeth.

"We'll move her to another department, so she doesn't have to face the man. Will that help?"

Cheng called Jackie as she was getting back to her office after lunch. She reached across the desk to grab the receiver.

"Five guys showed up for our little round table. Once we got them talking, there was no shutting them up. One after the other, they told stories about Shelton's creepy comments. How she would *accidentally* lock herself out of her room in the middle of the night when they were TDY and show up at their hotel room barely dressed." The disgust dripped from Cheng's words.

"Yuck."

"That was the general consensus. She's much older than most of these men—all enlisted, by the way."

"Wonder what she has against officers?" Jackie moved around the desk to sit and boot up her computer.

"Maybe she thinks enlisted guys are easier to manipulate. More willing to go along to get along."

"And how's that working for her?"

"Now that's someone's listening, and they know they aren't alone, they're ready to go on record."

"About time." As soon as the words left her mouth, she felt ashamed. She had a chance to speak up when she was a lieutenant and had elected to keep her mouth shut. She was in no position to judge.

"I heard the guys making plans to take Davies out to the enlisted club to show their support."

"Better late than never. How did it go with the wing commander?"

"He wants to talk to Davies, but I suggested he wait until the case is settled. He shouldn't get involved with anything ongoing."

"Good advice. Did he say anything about Shelton?" Jackie asked.

"Not really. I could tell he was skeptical at first, but he heard me out. When I told him a few of the things I found in such a short time, he was looking a little pale."

She snorted. "I wonder how deep Shelton's claws go."

"Apparently she's quite a name-dropper. A few of the guys said she offered favors for favors."

"Anything specific?"

"Nah, more like veiled innuendos. Back scratching and all that."

"Sleazy. So, what's your opinion? Could the wing commander be hiding anything?"

"Her boss? I think he's more worried about how this is going to tarnish his chance for promotion."

After the call, Jackie decided she had enough time to grab a coffee before her next meeting. She shot off a quick text to Leon and started down the stairs.

He met up with her in line at Starbucks. "An afternoon coffee? That might throw off your schedule."

She smiled. "I'm celebrating a partial win. Hopefully the first step on the road to victory."

"Webster?"

"No, this was the McGuire case. Cheng's down there and handling matters quite nicely."

"Well, good for you. I'm glad things are looking up."

They placed their orders and stood to the side to wait.

"When do you get your cast off?" Leon knocked lightly on the plaster.

Jackie swung her arm out of his reach. Her cast had been decorated by the soccer team. They thought it was cool that she had been hit by a car but didn't understand why she didn't get grounded for riding her bike on the street.

"Hopefully I'll get to have a removable cast soon. I'm a fast healer."

They retrieved their drinks when their names were called, and Jackie led them to a table.

"I'm kind of getting used to the cast, although I won't miss the itching. Short hair sure makes getting ready for work a lot faster."

"I could have told you that." Leon sipped his coffee. "What's going on with Webster?"

"Sergeant Renko is helping me. He sent me a list of folks who have left Webster's squadrons out of rotation. You know, like an early transfer. Renko's setting up meetings this afternoon so we can talk to some of them."

"What are you hoping for?"

"We'll see if they have anything to share about what it's

like to be under Webster's command. Maybe they'll all say he's a great guy."

"Or maybe they won't. Do you want to make a bet?"

"Leon, how unprofessional of you!" Jackie's mock scolding didn't faze him.

"Yeah, but do you? I think they'll tell you they got away as fast as they could."

She smiled but refused to take the bet. "We'll see. But I have to be careful not to lead them with my questions. It's going to be tough to hold my tongue."

"You're talking to guys too, right? Not just women?"

"Yes, we'll talk to both. For this first round, it'll depend on who is in the area. Then we'll decide whether or not to branch out."

Leon tipped his cup to finish the last dregs. "I need to get back to work. See you at practice."

Jackie felt reenergized and ready for her next challenge.

And it met her as soon as she entered the office.

Renko was waiting for her with paper in hand. "I found some things I thought you should see."

"I'm listening."

He put papers on her desk, pointing out sections as he spoke. "I noticed Sergeant Preston was on the report for Colonel Webster's first case. It didn't register immediately because he was only a character witness, not the first sergeant or anything. Then I saw his name again at the next base."

Turning the pages, he produced a summary of assignments for Preston. He laid the same report next to it with Webster's information on it. "They've been at every duty station together since that first report. Sometimes the timing is lagging for Preston, but he has been in Webster's squadron at each base."

"That's really unusual with the number of security forces squadrons we have."

"I agree, so I called the detailers at the personnel center. Seems Webster has requested Preston every time."

"That's interesting. When I asked Preston about how long he had been with Webster, he said he got to the base shortly after Webster."

Renko compared the duty assignments. "He wasn't lying. He didn't get to Andrews until after Webster, but he didn't really answer the question, did he? He's known him for several assignments now."

"Do you think he could be part of the problem?"

"You mean looking away when Webster plays his games instead of taking care of his troops? Sounds like all kinds of wrong."

Something niggled at the edge of Jackie's mind, but she couldn't quite catch sight of it. What was Webster getting out of all this? And why would Preston help?

Renko broke into her contemplations. "I've reserved the conference room so you could talk to some of the folks here in the building who've been in Webster's squadron. We should get going."

He led Jackie to a conference room off the fourth corridor. When they arrived, a staff sergeant was waiting outside.

"I'm sorry we're late," Jackie said, offering her hand.

"You're not late. I'm always early. I wasn't sure what I was walking into."

"That sounds ominous. This is only a conversation. No one's in trouble."

"No offense, ma'am, but I've heard that before."

Jackie led the young lady into the conference room, and they took seats at the table. Renko sat at the other end.

"I'm really glad you took the time to talk to me, but I'm concerned about your hesitation," Jackie said. "What happened to make you uneasy?"

The staff sergeant picked at the sleeve of her uniform. "Ma'am, you asked to talk to me about my time in Colonel Webster's unit. You must know, I left the squadron under a cloud."

"What kind of cloud?"

Staff Sergeant Morgan gave her a quizzical look. "My squadron hated me."

That caught Jackie by surprise. "Why would they hate you?"

"Your guess is as good as mine. The guys refused to talk to me, the few women in the squadron blamed me for making their life hell, and the commander was pissed because I wasn't onboard with his witch hunt."

"Witch hunt?"

"Ma'am, why am I here?"

"I'm sorry. I thought Sergeant Renko explained. I'm talking to people who I hope will give me some insight into what it's like under Colonel Webster's command."

"What are you hoping to find?"

"I don't have an agenda. I want the truth."

"The truth is, Colonel Webster makes up his own truth. If things don't fit his perception, he twists them until they do."

Jackie was speechless. She suspected there was a problem, but she had no idea it was this bad.

"Ma'am, I'm sorry if that wasn't what you were looking for, but I can't spin it another way."

"No. I'm not looking for a spin, I assure you. Can you tell me what happened?"

"One day I got called into the commander's office. He heard I had a run-in with one of the other cops—a male cop. It was no big deal, so I was a little disconcerted that he knew about it."

"Do you mind telling me what it was about?"

Morgan crossed her legs and got comfortable. "Not at all. A guy asked me out. I said no. That should have been the end of it. Next thing I know, the commander's giving me the third degree about not putting up with pressure from men. It was like Colonel Webster wanted me to say something happened that didn't. It really was no big deal. When I told the guy no, he was cool about it. Until after my meeting with Webster. Then he refused to talk to me. He and his buddies iced me. Even got up and moved away when I sat down. Really stupid if you ask me."

Jackie took in the information. *Why would Webster get involved with something as minor as a spurned invitation?* "Did the guy outrank you?"

"No, ma'am. He was the same as me. We were in the same tech training."

"And there was no bad blood between you?"

"Not until after the commander got involved. When I refused to make a complaint, Colonel Webster was a bit of an ass, if you don't mind me saying. He was really condescending. Acting like he was trying to help me when all he really did was make the guys stop talking to me. That's tough in a cop squadron. Once you're ghosted, you're pretty much done. What else are you going to do if guys won't work with you?"

Jackie remembered her own struggle in the missile launch world when men had a choice whether or not to pull an alert with a woman, but she didn't have the same choice. It was a tough position to be in.

"What did you do?"

"I transferred as soon as I could. There are plenty of jobs here in the Pentagon. They aren't glorious, and I'm stuck behind a desk, but at least I'm away from the whispers. I've even reconnected with some of the guys from the squadron. Once they took the time to listen to my side of the story, they realized it was a misunderstanding. I never said a negative word against any member of my unit."

Jackie handed the staff sergeant a business card. "You can get in touch with me if you think of anything else. I may reach out again, if that's all right."

"Of course. I'm not sure what you're up to, but I'll do what I can for you."

Morgan left, and Renko brought in the next interviewee. The story was very similar, but this time, from the other perspective.

"I had no idea why I was called into the commander's office. I didn't think it was a crime to hit on a member of my unit. She started the flirting to begin with." Staff Sergeant Nusbic shifted uncomfortably in his seat. Sweat beaded on his forehead. He was obviously not over the distress inflicted by the accusation.

"And you never said or did anything to give this woman the wrong impression?"

"Ma'am, I was never even alone with her—ever. We were on different shifts. I thought she was pretty and all but nothing worth ruining my career over."

"Why did he call you in?"

"He gave me a lecture about how to treat women. How they were to be treasured and all that. I'm from the south. My daddy drilled that into my head when I was young. I didn't know what I did wrong or what Colonel Webster was talking about." He wiped his palm across his forehead and then dried his hand on his pants.

"What did you do after that meeting?"

"I got out of that squadron as fast as I could. Afterward, Emily—that was the girl I was flirting with—called me. She swore she never talked to the commander or said anything bad about me. I believe her. She's not that kind of a person."

Jackie tilted her head. "Did you ever mention the commander's behavior to anyone higher up the chain?"

"Me? As an airman at the time, calling the group commander? I don't think so. I was glad to get out of there with my career intact. I got a letter of admonishment, but that went away after six months. Everything's going great now."

The next person Jackie spoke with told an eerily parallel tale. Jackie was having a hard time reconciling this version of Webster with the one Buckley had fawned over. She had to ask about it.

"Do you know Sergeant Buckley? She speaks very highly of Colonel Webster."

"Yeah, I know Buckley. She's a little whacked, if you don't mind me saying." The technical sergeant was relaxed talking about Webster and their prior interactions. Enough years had passed, and his career seemed to be on a steady uphill climb.

"What do you mean?"

"When she found out I had been in Webster's squadron—he was only a major when I knew him—she went on and on—all dreamy-like—about how great he was. When I said I wasn't so sure about that, she went off. Just like that." He clasped his hands in his lap. His legs bounced as he lifted and dropped his heels.

"Went off?"

"Started telling me I didn't know what I was talking about. Said how great Webster is. I don't think we could have been talking about the same guy. Or maybe he's that much better to the women under his command." He looked at his watch. "Ma'am, do you mind if I cut out of here? I want to catch the next train home."

"No, of course not. Thanks for talking to me."

All the transferees she had talked to had basically the same story. Webster was an okay guy, but the men were nervous around him, waiting for the other shoe to drop. They were afraid to be seen with the women in the squadron in case they were accused of something inappropriate. It wasn't good for morale and many people—men and women—transferred out as soon as they could.

She turned to Renko. "What do you think?"

"I wouldn't want to be in his unit."

"Me either."

"Want me to set up some more interviews? We can call them if they aren't nearby. There are a few at Andrews still, just in special duties."

"Yes, please. I'm missing something. Maybe getting more perspectives will help." Jackie straightened her notes and picked them up with her good hand.

"I have a question," Renko said. "Why isn't Preston afraid to be in the same squadron as Webster?"

Chapter 35

I got here as soon as I could." Jackie wrapped her good arm around her sister.

"You didn't have to Uber. I would have picked you up." Alison took the handle of Jackie's suitcase.

Jackie froze, giving Alison a dubious look.

"Okay, so I would have sent Lance." The sisters laughed and hugged again.

"I'm putting you right next to the baby's room so you can get up with her in the night." Alison rolled the suitcase into the guest room.

"It's perfect. Though I'm not sure I can help with what she really needs. When do I get to meet my niece?"

"As soon as Lance is willing to give her up," Alison said. "I'm so glad you could get away."

"I told you I would. I just needed to hand off some things so someone else could cover for me while I'm gone."

"How's your arm?"

"Itches a bit. Can't wait to get rid of this thing."

"Any updates from the police?"

"No. I've called a few times, but they just keep repeating there's nothing to go on."

"What about Ring cameras on the neighbor's doors?"

Jackie laughed. "Are you turning into a detective now?"

"I've seen it on TV shows."

"Actually, they did check. Not a lot of houses on that street use a service like that. But a good thought. Keep them coming."

Jackie washed her hands in the kitchen sink, careful to keep her cast dry. Then she sprayed it with a misting hand sanitizer. "Where's Lance? I want to hold that baby."

Alison linked her arm in Jackie's and led her into the nursery. Teddy bears floating in hot air balloons made a splash of color on the wall's gender-neutral yellow paint.

Lance stood at the changing table. "I thought I heard your voice." He gave her a peck on the cheek while keeping a hand on the baby.

Jackie wrapped a burp cloth around her cast, then playfully shoved Lance away from the baby. "Here's the real person I came to see."

Alison settled the warm bundle on Jackie's padded arm, supporting the baby's neck with the crook of the cast as Jackie tucked her closer. "Hello, little one. Aunt Jackie's here. We're going to have so much fun!"

"I'll let you two bond. I'm going to clean up." Lance left the women alone in the nursery.

Alison watched Jackie. "Are you okay?"

Rocking the baby in her arms, Jackie kissed the tiny forehead and absorbed her scent. "Why wouldn't I be?"

"I know how much you wanted kids."

Jackie shrugged, still staring at the newborn. "It wasn't meant to be. That doesn't mean I'm not thrilled to death for you. And I am going to spoil Harper Leigh rotten."

"It's not too late, you know." Alison placed an arm around Jackie's waist.

A bitter laugh escaped her lips. "Maybe if I had a one-night stand tomorrow."

"Don't give up. You have so much love to give."

"Then you better have another baby, so I don't overwhelm this one."

Chapter 36

Jackie put her phone in speaker mode and dialed Leon's number. Once it started ringing, she continued rolling her suitcase toward her apartment. The thump-thump-thump over the wooden deck boards sounded loud in the otherwise quiet, evening air.

"I'm back. How did the game go?" Jackie asked Leon when he answered.

"Hectic. But did you expect anything less? How's your sister?"

"Mom and baby are both doing well. My brother-in-law is going to have his hands full trying to keep up with that little princess."

"Where are you now? Do you need a ride from the airport?"

"No, I took the Metro. I'm walking up to my door now. Give me a second."

She dug her key out of her pocket and slipped it in the lock. "Did Colonel Dellinger—" Her words cut off abruptly.

"Jackie? Hey? Are you still there?"

"Dammit!"

"What's wrong?"

"Someone broke into my apartment!"

"Get out of there!" Leon yelled.

Jackie stood quietly, listening. "I don't think anyone is still here."

"Don't go inside! I'm on my way over. Call the police!"

"I'm fine. No one's here." She walked around the debris scattered across the floor, stepping over a broken framed picture of her and Stan. The door to her bedroom stood partially ajar. She pushed it with her foot, but something behind the door kept it from fully opening. Peeking around the door, she saw piles of clothes blocking her way. The mattress was tipped on its side, and her bedside clock was shattered.

"Are you listening to me?"

"I am, Leon. I'm going to call the cops right now. Don't bother coming over, but I'll probably need a place to stay tonight."

"Are you sure you don't want me to come over?"

"I'm sure. What could you do anyway? Let Vicki know I wanted a sleepover. I'll call you when I'm on my way."

She disconnected and called 911. Within five minutes, two police officers were at her apartment. Jackie was waiting outside, pacing back and forth. The nametag on the shorter man read Washington, while the tall officer's said Liu.

"You called about a break-in?"

After giving them her information, she led them into the apartment. Liu looked around the living room while Washington peeled off to inspect the other rooms.

"What time did you leave the apartment?"

"Actually, I've been gone a week. I was on leave at my sister's."

"And you left directly from here?"

She gave a rundown of her itinerary, and Lui added to his notepad.

"Is anything missing?" Liu asked.

"I don't know. I didn't go digging around yet."

Washington returned. "The bedroom windows are still locked."

"TV's still here. Looks like someone was looking for something specific," Lui said.

"I don't have anything hidden in my apartment." When she traveled, she always took her computer and her favorite jewelry. She said a silent prayer that her wedding ring was at her parents' house. She didn't own anything else of value.

"What about something from work?"

"I work at the Pentagon, but I don't bring anything important home with me. Certainly nothing classified." She briefly explained her office while Lui took notes.

"Does anyone else have access to this apartment? An ex maybe? Someone you gave a spare key to in case of emergencies?"

She shook her head. "The front office, obviously. I haven't given a key to anyone."

"Have you made any enemies that may have done this?" Lui asked.

Jackie couldn't help herself. She started laughing.

The officers exchanged a curious look.

She covered her mouth with a hand, trying to get her nervous laughter under control. "I'm sorry. It's just—" she broke off, not knowing where to start. "There's a lot going on right now. I probably have a lot of people who would like to make life hard for me, but I don't see the point of breaking into my apartment. It's not like I have anything anyone would be looking for."

"What happened to your arm?" Lui asked.

"Hit and run while I was on my bike."

"Think these incidents might be connected?" Washington asked.

"No telling." She fished out her wallet, fumbling to hold it with her casted hand while she pulled out a card. "This is the cop handling the accident investigation."

Lui copied down the info and handed it back.

"Do you have a place to stay? I'd like to send a tech team over to look around, but it would be better if we could wait until morning." Washington gave her a business card, and she passed him one of hers.

"Have them give me thirty minutes' warning before they head this way, and I'll meet them here. I'm going to stay with a friend tonight."

"We'll wait while you gather some things," Washington said.

Jackie gestured at her suitcase. "I already have a bag packed. I was just getting home."

"After the techs finish up tomorrow, please inventory your home and let us know if anything of value was taken," Washington said. "This could simply be a thief who noticed you were out of town and took advantage of the empty apartment."

The officers walked her to the garage and waited until she drove off.

Jackie was proud of herself for maintaining her calm, but now that she was alone, the tears blurred her vision. She wiped her eyes and pulled into the gas station at the entrance to the highway. Putting her car in park, she allowed herself to vent the anger, fear, and frustration she felt. She alternated between sobs and absurd laughter, thinking about everything that was going on. The break-in could be connected to one of her cases, or it could be her dumb luck.

When she felt she was cried out, she dried her eyes and put the car back into gear. As she drove to Leon's house, she said a prayer of thanks that she had been at her sisters.

Chapter 37

At the office early, Jackie went through the paperwork on her desk. She had kept up to date with her emails while her sister and Harper were napping, but some work still required old-fashioned signatures. When her boss came in, Jackie dutifully reported the break-in at her apartment and told her she was on call to meet up with the technicians.

"Do whatever you need to do. What a horrible thing to happen," Major General Varn said.

"But on a brighter note, the OSI investigation at McGuire has really stirred up some dirt on Ms. Shelton."

"I heard. The wing commander called to let me know he moved her into a special duty position while they finish up. She's claiming discrimination because she's female, saying the commander has had it out for her since he took over the wing."

Jackie gave Varn a quizzical look. "But he defended her."

"Truth is not the issue here. It's all about deflecting and passing the blame. The group commander has also been relieved of command for lack of confidence. He should have seen what was happening."

"And if OSI finds out he knew about Shelton's behavior and did nothing?"

"That will be another investigation with possibly dire consequences. I don't want to speculate."

"Well, the temporary SARC is in place at McGuire and has been following up with the complaints that were in the email queue. Hopefully she'll be able to reach some of the people with concerns and get the ball rolling. Then she can hand off to the full-time replacement."

"At least they'll know someone is listening now. Good job."

Jackie felt the rush that came with the compliment. As the child of an alcoholic, she was aware of her triggers and her rewards; acknowledgement for a job well done was all she needed.

"How are things at Andrews?"

"Sergeant Renko and I have been conducting interviews with people who transferred out of Webster's squadrons. They all say the same thing—Webster seems overly sensitive to women. Like in an unhealthy way."

"What do you want to do with that information?"

It felt like a test. Jackie wasn't sure what the general expected her to answer.

"There's no official investigation into Webster or his actions. At this point, no one is asking questions but us. If we drop it, nothing is going to happen. But if we get to a place where we can show suspected misconduct or at least get the IG or OSI interested, maybe they can investigate it and see if there is a problem."

"And what if they investigate and there isn't a problem?"

Deep in the pit of her soul, Jackie knew something wasn't right in Webster's squadron. But did she trust the system to ferret out the problem?

"I believe our questions will help people like Amanda Nelson and the men wrongly accused." Jackie met her boss's firm gaze and held it.

Varn shook her head. "I hope your instincts are right."

~

"You need to get a handle on your officer, general." The congressman's voice was raspy though he tried to sound intimidating.

Major General Varn sat stiffly in the chair beside Jackie in the congressman's office. The general's usually confident demeanor took on an icy edge not quite reaching hostile. She let the man's comment slide off her.

Major Wilson stood at a casual parade rest against one wall, trying to blend into the paneling.

Olan sat heavily back in his chair. "First, she goes after a young, enlisted man who doesn't know any better and deserves a second chance. Now she is on a witch hunt at McGuire; going after a woman, no less! What is wrong with her? She wouldn't know sexual assault if it was happening to her!"

Major General Varn cut a glance at Jackie. Jackie counted slowly to calm herself.

Varn stood and Jackie followed her lead. "I know you're busy, congressman, so we won't take up any more of your time."

"You wait one minute. You haven't told me what you're going to do to fix this situation."

"I will look over Lieutenant Colonel Austin's work thoroughly and ensure she is upholding the standards we expect from Air Force officers."

"You best do that! And she owes Ms. Shelton a public apology." He shuffled papers on his desk and muttered under his breath, "Putting her through such an ordeal."

Jackie followed the general out of the office, not having uttered a single word during the visit. Major Wilson kept a respectful distance. When they reached the wide, marble hallway, Major General Varn visibly shook off the tension she had been holding. They followed Wilson out of the building into the humid air and heat rising from the sidewalks. Neither woman spoke until they got on the shuttle to take them back to the Pentagon.

"Ma'am," Jackie started, but the general cut her off with a raised hand.

"Do your job. Don't worry about people like this who get in your way. Dealing with them is my job."

Jackie stared out the window as the sky opened up, releasing huge raindrops. The suppressed energy she had been withholding rushed out of her, washed away by the rain.

Chapter 38

The hairs on the back of her neck were standing up. Jackie had made the walk from the grocery store to her apartment many times before, but for some reason, this felt different.

The sun had set hours ago, and the streetlamps were casting shadows across the sidewalk.

Jackie stopped to shift her bags awkwardly from one shoulder to the other. Although the cast had been removed and replaced with a removable one, she still couldn't carry groceries with her left arm. That made this routine trek feel so much longer.

As she began again, a sound caught her attention. *Was that a foot shuffling?* She snuck a peek over her shoulder. Nothing.

She turned the corner. Her apartment was within sight. Just a few more blocks. Tonight, the walk from the grocery store was taking longer than usual.

There it was again. Jackie stopped to look in the window of a closed storefront. She'd seen this done before on TV. She adjusted her eyes to look at the reflection in the glass. That might be a person behind that parked truck, but she couldn't be sure.

After a few minutes, she felt silly and continued her journey. This time, she was sure she heard footsteps.

She didn't want someone to follow her home. If something was going to happen, she needed it to be here, where at least some people were within yelling distance.

Acting as if she forgot something, Jackie turned on her heels and retraced her route. She walked quickly, leaving plenty of room on the sidewalk between her and the parked cars.

A shadow stood frozen between a truck and an SUV. As Jackie came alongside him, her heart raced, but she knew this man had been following her, and she couldn't let him get away with it.

She spun to confront him. For a moment, she was too stunned to speak. Then the anger returned.

"Why are you following me?" she demanded.

Webster held his hands out as if to hold her at bay. "It's not what you think."

"You have no idea what I think!"

"I'm not here to hurt you."

"Then why are you following me?" she repeated.

"I'm worried about you."

Jackie scoffed. "Why would *you* be worried about *me*?"

"Last time I saw you, you were upset. I don't mean to be indelicate, but I noticed the bruises. And of course the cast. I want to help."

"You could help by leaving me alone. Following me is creepy."

"I didn't mean to scare you. I wanted to make sure you were all right."

"How did you find me?"

He looked intently at his shoes.

"Answer me! How long have you been following me?"

"I saw you leave work. You really should be more mindful of your surroundings, if you don't mind me saying."

"I do mind! If you come near me again, we won't be having a conversation. You'll be picking your teeth off the ground."

"Come on now. You're overreacting." A smile played across his face.

"You better leave right now or I'm calling the cops." She pulled her cell phone from her jacket pocket.

Holding his hands up again, he backed away. Then, without another word, he turned and walked back the way he'd come.

Jackie watched him go. The adrenaline that had been coursing through her body left her all at once, and she started to tremble.

She fell against the wall and let it hold her up until Webster turned the corner. Then she wasted no more time getting to her apartment, looking over her shoulder every few yards.

Chapter 39

As Jackie rode the bus to work the next morning, she wrestled with whether she should tell Colonel Dellinger about her run-in with Webster.

Of course Leon was no help. When she had told him, he wanted her to call the cops. He was overprotective at times. She didn't want to cry wolf when it wasn't needed.

And Jackie knew if she told her boss, Varn would also call Dellinger.

She didn't want to make a big deal about it and come across as a complainer, but she also knew Webster had a problem. *Had he done this to other women?*

Part of her wondered if she was looking for an excuse to see Colonel Dellinger again. But that was ridiculous.

Why did he come see her at the hospital if he was married? What was he thinking?

He is a genuinely nice guy who cares for his troops, Jackie argued with herself. *He was just looking out for me.*

She reached the Pentagon, followed the stream of people through the turnstiles, and swiped her badge. Pinning it to her uniform, she was pulled along by the morning rush. As she waited to get on the escalator, she caught sight of Sergeant Buckley staring at her. Jackie gave a small nod in acknowledgement. Buckley didn't smile or nod, but she didn't break eye contact either. She continued to regard Jackie with something close to contempt.

Stepping onto the moving staircase, Jackie disregarded the encounter with a shake of her head, already thinking about what the day would bring.

Two notes were stuck to her monitor, where she couldn't miss them. One from Captain Corbin. She began there, dialing before even turning on her computer. She plopped down into her chair.

"Whatever you did shook things up here," Captain Corbin said.

"My boss is a formidable person. Seeing her dress-down Erin's director scared me. I'm not going to get on her bad side."

"Well, the talk of a deal has stopped. Or at least the idea of Kirkson staying in the Air Force is off the table. We'll see what his lawyer comes up with next, but at least he'll have to work for his money."

"What does Erin think of all this?"

"She's grateful that he's being punished. She wasn't looking forward to going to court, but she wasn't going to let him get away with what happened to her."

After they hung up, Jackie took the time to power up her computer while she read the second note left for her. Removing the sticky, she was grateful whoever took the message had included Wilson's number, so she didn't have to look it up.

She placed the call to Wilson's office.

"I did a little digging into the Kirkson properties. Looks like they aren't on very solid footing after all," Wilson said. "They made a series of bad investments. Seems like they were counting on rezoning efforts that fell through. To top it off, the business manager they hired was lining his own pockets. Now he's skipped the country."

"Does that mean Representative Olan won't be getting his campaign contribution?"

"I can't imagine how. Even selling their first-born won't bring in much cash."

"I wonder if the congressman knows."

"I doubt it. I don't think he'd be spending this much time on the Kirksons if he did."

"What time? I've only seen Olan once. We've been updating his staffer."

"That's typical. Don't get discouraged. The staffers really have all the power anyway. They're the gatekeepers."

"I just spoke with Captain Corbin at Wright-Pat." Jackie caught Wilson up on the details.

"Looks like the tightrope that kid's been walking is coming unraveled," Wilson said.

Chapter 40

While the kids cheered and chased the soccer ball around, Jackie couldn't stop herself from sneaking glances at the bleachers.

"Who are you looking for?" Leon asked.

"No one."

"Well, he isn't here yet."

Jackie shot him a look. "What does that mean?"

He laughed. "Nothing. You're so uptight. What's gotten into you?"

She shook her head. "Got a lot going on."

"Or maybe not enough."

"What are you talking about?"

"You need a date."

She blanched.

"I know it's been a while, and I'm saying this as a dear friend with your best interests at heart. You need to get back out there. When was the last time you went on a date?"

She didn't even have to think about it. "It was with Stan."

He put an arm around her shoulders. "It's time."

Brushing him off, she clapped her right hand against her leg and cheered as one of the children kicked the ball hard down the field.

"There's a guy in my office. He's only a major, but he's a

hard worker. Definitely going places. Recently divorced. Seems like a nice guy. Want me to introduce you?"

She glowered at him. "I don't need your matchmaking skills, thank you."

"What about Webster? With his overprotective nature, he'd probably make a great boyfriend."

"Very funny."

"But really, you need to get out more. Working with the kids is great, but now it's time to step up your game."

"Your wife can't get home soon enough. Maybe she can get you to stop meddling in my life."

"Who do you think recommended the major?"

Leon redirected Vicki, who had stopped to pick flowers on the side of the field. She ran toward the ball, dandelions clutched in her chubby hand.

The referee blew a whistle, signaling the end of the first half. The kids charged the bench, ready for their midgame snack. Jackie passed out bags of apple slices as quickly as she could, trying to keep the kids from running into her soft cast. Leon tried to impart his soccer wisdom on the first graders, but it was lost in lieu of juice boxes.

When the whistle blew again, the children ran back onto the field, leaving Jackie feeling as she had been hit by a whirlwind.

She was so happy, swept up in the craziness that was children on a sunny day. Watching them run, tumble, fall, and pick themselves back up again gave her a feeling of peace.

"Good shot, Kendra!"

The voice made Jackie's heart skip a beat. Trying not to look obvious, she turned her head to the stands. Colonel Dellinger stood at the bottom of the bleachers, clapping and cheering his daughter on.

Jackie's heart ached.

Chapter 41

After another late night at work, Jackie found herself disembarking the bus on automatic pilot. She adjusted the backpack on her left shoulder.

She raised her hood against the drizzle and tucked her cast inside her jacket. Even the soft cast gave off a nasty smell when it got wet. Casually, she glanced around. The weather had mostly cleared the streets. A splash from behind caught her attention. Instinctively, she felt for the pepper spray she had started carrying in her pocket. Finding nothing, she cursed the Pentagon's ban against bringing in anything that could be considered a weapon—even personal safety devices. She calculated the distance to the nearest open store.

Then she sensed him, too close. Instead of fear, rage lit behind her eyes.

When she felt his hand on her shoulder, she stopped suddenly and spun around. "I warned you!" She jabbed her right fist, connecting with his jaw in a satisfying crunch.

She stumbled back. As quickly as the righteous anger had overtaken her, horror at what she had done paralyzed her. This was not Colonel Webster.

The man regained his balance and lunged for her with both hands. When he grabbed the front of her jacket, she immediately responded, snaking both her arms up and through his, then driving down hard with her elbows, breaking his hold. A searing pain shot through her left arm. Pushing past the pain, she kicked out with her right foot, just missing his groin.

He made another grab, catching the cast on her left arm. She screamed as she grappled to get loose, but the rain muffled her cry.

She spun her arm in a circle, trying to get free. As the move pulled him in closer, she put the power of her right elbow into his face.

A horn blared. Lights flashed. Something large barreled toward them on the sidewalk.

The figure released Jackie and ran, stumbling on the rain-soaked pavement.

The car stopped feet in front of her. Webster got out and raced to her side. "Are you all right? Did he hurt you?"

~

"When I was in college, a friend of mine was raped." Webster slowly spun the water glass between his hands, not meeting Jackie's eyes.

After the police had responded to the 911 call about Jackie's attacker, she and Webster had made statements and were released. Now they sat in a dimly lit restaurant amongst diners who were oblivious to the strained conversation unfolding.

Jackie remained silent, not wanting to intrude on his memory.

"She told me one night after a lot of beer. I didn't know what to say." He stared off into the distance.

"I wanted to help her—I really did. I didn't know how." His voice dropped to a whisper. "The next night, she overdosed on some drug she got at a frat party."

Jackie's hand reflexively covered her mouth. "That's horrible."

"When the cops came by to question her friends, no one mentioned the rape, so I didn't either. I figured her girlfriends had to know before I did, and if they didn't tell, it must have been for a good reason. I didn't want to shame her. She was dead now; what did it matter?" Webster took a sip of water.

"It wasn't your fault."

"The rape wasn't, but I could have stopped the overdose. If I had only done something. If I had offered to help. She might still be here."

"There was no way for you to know what she was going to do."

"But what if I had insisted she go to the police? What if I had taken her to the hospital?"

"She still might have not wanted to face it." Jackie's voice was soft.

"But I'll never know, will I?"

Jackie didn't know how to respond. It was easy to second guess him after the fact, but that wasn't fair.

Webster must have sensed her thoughts. "I know. I didn't even try to help her. Then after she died, I didn't want people to know that I might have stopped her. I took the coward's way out and kept quiet. I've begged for her forgiveness over and over in my prayers. I swore to her memory that I would never let something like that happen again."

He looked into Jackie's eye for the first time since he started talking. "I won't keep silent again. Someone needs to stand up and protect those women."

Chapter 42

Jackie looked over her notes. What if Webster wasn't the bastard she thought he was? Misogynistic, yes. But could he simply be misguided in his attempts to help?

A knock caused her to look up.

"Colonel Dellinger, what are you doing here?" Jackie stood at her desk in the Pentagon. The last place she expected to see him on a Friday morning.

"I had a meeting in the building. Thought I'd stop by to see if you had time for coffee."

Jackie stared at him.

"Jackie? Are you okay?"

"Uh, yes, sir. Sure. Let's get coffee." She pulled her ID from the computer to lock it and followed him out of the office and toward the closest coffee stand.

"I see you got your cast off. How does it feel?"

"Pretty good. A little sore today, but overall, better." *Why is he checking on me?*

"Colonel Webster told me what happened last night. And how he happened to be there," Dellinger said.

"He did?"

"Why didn't you?"

"Well, I, I wasn't sure of the protocol in this situation."

"Did you tell General Varn?"

"She's out of the office all day. I'll let her know when she gets back."

"You're playing a dangerous game."

"And I seem to be losing." Jackie laughed.

"This isn't a laughing matter."

"I'm sorry, sir."

He sighed. "I'm not mad. I'm worried about you. This, after someone already hit you with a car. It can't be a coincidence."

Her face grew hot; she tried to cool it with the touch of her hand.

"I'm leaning toward issuing Colonel Webster a no contact order with you, but he did stop the attack so now I'm not sure what to do."

They ordered their coffee and found a table.

Jackie took a sip and thought about what he had said. "I'm also torn. I swear Webster's up to something. Why else would he be following me? But he obviously isn't the one who attacked me, so I must have pissed someone else off."

Dellinger grinned. "Not you."

Jackie's face went red again.

"What else are you involved with?"

Her mind initially heard the question as *who else are you involved with*. Then she shook her head, trying not to think of Colonel Dellinger as anyone but a commander doing his job.

She blew out a breath and explained the call she had received from Erin Mollner and how Varn had gone off on the director at Wright-Patterson.

Dellinger shook his head in disgust. "I'm not sure how those dinosaur-thinkers are still working for the Air Force."

"I don't think he will be for long. General Varn called his boss as soon as we got off the phone. She made me leave for that conversation."

"Good for her." Dellinger's drawl was more pronounced when he smiled.

Then she gave him a quick rundown on the Davies case, including how the SARC totally mishandled the case.

"Where's the lieutenant now?"

"I'm not sure. She was relieved of her position, but I don't know where they moved her."

"I'll call the McGuire wing commander and ask."

"Won't that look strange? Why would you care or even know about it?"

He shrugged it off. "He's a friend of mine. He won't care why I want to know."

"You have to be careful asking about Ms. Shelton though. If the rumors are true, she has pull in a lot of places. I'd hate for you to get blackballed on account of me."

When he smiled this time, Jackie's legs went weak; she was glad she was seated. "I'm just saying . . ."

"You're worried about me now? Don't be. I've faced off civilians before. It may not be pleasant, but it's doable."

Chapter 43

Theresa caught Jackie in the stairwell of her apartment complex. "You got your cast off! That's great."

"It makes showering much easier, that's for sure. I have to wear this removable one for a few weeks, but it's healing."

"Still no bike riding, huh?"

"Not yet. I've been researching which new bike to get."

"I'm meeting some of the ladies tonight. Want to go with us? We're going to a new club."

Jackie shook her head. "I'm not a club-goer."

Theresa's face fell.

"How about a compromise? Let's pregame at my place," Jackie said.

The usual pep returned to Theresa, and she clapped her hands. "Really? That would be so much fun! What can I bring? Oh, I need to text the girls. Everyone can bring something. What time? Not too late. We want to be able to get into the club. I hear the live band is to die for."

Jackie laughed at her enthusiasm. "Eight? Would that work? Bring whatever you want. I have wine, that's about it."

"You got it. See you at eight." She gave Jackie a quick, tight squeeze and was off.

Jackie was still smiling when she unlocked her apartment door. Usually there was just a moment before the door swung open when she was apprehensive, expecting the mess she'd encountered when she returned from Alison's house. This time she walked through the door light-hearted. Theresa had that effect on her. She needed to make more of an effort to hang out with her.

After the police techs had taken fingerprints and checked the locks on Jackie's apartment, she had done a deep clean as she put everything back in order. Nothing appeared to be stolen. Even her TV and stereo were untouched. The place was just a mess—broken glass, slashed pillows, and upturned drawers. Even Stan's cereal had been opened and flung across the room. She took the opportunity to purge things from her past.

She peered at her wrist, searching for her watch. Instead, the soft cast taunted her. She looked up at the clock in the kitchen instead. Plenty of time to change and grab something to eat before the ladies arrived.

At seven on the dot, Theresa showed up with a grocery bag of chips and assorted dips in one hand and bottles clicking together in the other. Jackie helped her get everything to the counter safely and pulled out glasses for Theresa to start mixing her brew.

She spoke almost nonstop about work, a new guy at the gym, and about how much fun they were going to have tonight. She asked Jackie about the soccer team and her new niece. By the time the other ladies arrived around seven-thirty, Jackie had downed two of Theresa's Calimochos and was working on her third. The iced mixture of red wine and soda went down too easily.

While the ladies caught up on gossip and talked about people Jackie didn't know, her mind drifted back to work.

"How does a self-righteous guy who is so condescending to women get promoted?"

Theresa stopped midstory to look at Jackie.

"I mean, why does the Air Force reward him for doing what any decent person should be doing anyway? Not the condescending part. The taking care of his troops part. No one should be sexually assaulted—EVER. But they think he's a hero because he prosecuted the guy who did the assault? What about stopping it from happening in the first place?"

"How many of those drinks did you give her?" Anne asked Theresa.

Theresa was giggling. "I'm not sure, but she needs another one." She jumped up and weaved her way to the kitchen to mix another.

Jackie went on as if no one had said anything. "He keeps getting promoted. And the slimy first sergeant just holds on to his coattails. Getting promoted even faster than Webster."

Something clicked in Jackie's alcohol-addled brain.

Chapter 44

You know Lieutenant Colonel Austin, don't you?" Colonel Dellinger asked Sergeant Preston after they had all been seated in the wing commander's office.

Preston nodded at Jackie.

"Then let's get down to it. We need your help."

"My help, sir?"

"Colonel Austin has convinced me the number of SAPR reports out of the security forces squadron is excessive."

Preston blanched.

"I know you're loyal to your commander, and that's commendable. But you should know, we believe Colonel Webster has been filing false reports for some reason. We're not sure what he gets out of it. Colonel Austin speculates some type of Messiah complex, but I'm not convinced yet. We were hoping you could shed some light on it."

Preston licked his lips nervously. His eyes darted around the room as if looking for his next sentence.

"Has Colonel Webster been filing reports with no backing?" Jackie asked.

His eyes fixed on her. "Ma'am, I'm not sure what you want me to say."

"We only want the truth. Do you have any thoughts about the numerous cases brought forth?"

He squirmed uncomfortably in his chair. "Colonel Webster is a good boss. He cares about his troops."

"There's no doubt about that," Dellinger said. "But that doesn't explain over reporting SAPR cases."

"I had nothing to do with that, sir."

Dellinger gave a dismissive gesture. "We just want to get Colonel Webster the help he needs. As a matter of fact, I have a position opening on the wing staff very soon. I can make sure you aren't in the frag pattern when this all comes to light."

Preston sat straighter in his seat. "Sir, I don't want to talk poorly about a superior officer."

"I'm asking you directly."

"I have raised my concerns with Colonel Webster with this issue."

"How did he respond?"

"He didn't want to listen. He takes any slight against a woman very seriously. Almost to the point of fixation. I'm a little worried about him."

"Did you put any of your concerns in writing?"

"In writing, sir?"

Dellinger leaned both elbows on his desk, interlocking his fingers. "Just notes about when you talked to him, a basic rundown of what was said, that kind of thing. It doesn't have to be anything formal."

"Well, I wasn't sure of anything, and I didn't want to get him in trouble. Everyone looks up to him."

"I understand that. We're not trying to get him in trouble either. At this point, we don't even know if he's done anything wrong."

His eyes found a spot above Dellinger's head. "I have been keeping a log of our discussions since I became concerned about the number of reports. I'm not sure why. I just thought it was important to track so that I could talk to him about it if . . . "

"If you noticed a trend?" Jackie finished for him.

"Yes, ma'am."

"Where is this log?"

"It's on my computer at work."

"Can you send me a copy?" Dellinger asked.

Preston licked his lips again. Then he looked at his watch.

"It doesn't have to be tonight. I realize it's the end of the day. First thing in the morning will be fine."

"Thank you, sir. I do have plans tonight, but I can email you in the morning."

Chapter 45

At the office, Jackie answered the phone automatically. When the special cadence of his voice reached her, Colonel Dellinger had all her attention.

"I forgot to tell you yesterday, with everything else going on. I talked to my buddy at McGuire. The SARC there has been moved to the services squadron. Probably handing out basketballs at the gym now."

"She can't do much damage there," Jackie said.

"She's also put in her papers," Dellinger added.

"With all the heat surrounding Shelton, the writing's on the wall. O'Connor is probably trying to get out before they find something to charge her with and kick her out."

The sound of clicking came through the receiver. "I received an email from Sergeant Preston this morning. I'm sending it to you now. Take a look at it and let me know what you think," he said.

They disconnected and Jackie waited for the email. When it popped up, she downloaded the attachment, then looked at the file properties. The document was created five months ago.

She opened it and scanned through the information. It was rough dates and times of conversations between Webster and Preston, with short comments and musings. Preston had also made reminders for himself to follow up on one point or another. Jackie would have to read through the document more thoroughly, but for now, she jotted off a quick confirmation of receipt email to Colonel Dellinger.

Turning to a fresh sheet in her notebook, Jackie made notes as she read through the Preston file. He seemed to have covered all the bases, noting his objections for each case. In this document, he didn't come across as the firm supporter of Webster as commander of the year as he did in person.

She wondered if Colonel Dellinger noticed this as well.

When she finished her reading, she went back and crosschecked the notes against the reports that were made. Each one was covered. Interestingly, there weren't any that *weren't* mentioned. Meaning Webster did not once take the advice of his trusted first sergeant, but the shirt still spoke very highly of him.

Why?

Chapter 46

We would love to have you and Coach Leon over for dinner to thank you for all the time you put in with the kids," Dellinger said to Jackie after soccer practice.

"That's really not necessary." The last thing she wanted to do was spend the evening watching him with Veronica when she was still struggling to get over the excitement his southern drawl stirred in her.

"We insist. Besides, Kendra has been asking to invite Vicki over anyway."

Jackie searched for a way out of her predicament but couldn't think of anything. "I'll talk to Leon and see what he says. It's a really nice gesture and not at all required."

"Not a problem. Let me know if next weekend will work for you both."

Jackie watched as he joined Kendra and Veronica. The little girl held the hands of the adults, picking up her feet so they would swing her between them. Jackie's heart broke a little at the happy sight, once again reminded of the children she would never have.

A thump in the center of her back brought her back to the present. Turning, she picked up the soccer ball Leon had hit her with and whipped it back at him.

He dodged, knocking the ball aside. "These things aren't going to magically get put away while you're making moon eyes at the commander, you know."

"What are you talking about?"

He laughed. "Really? You're going to play dumb with me?"

Jackie concentrated on picking up the balls, tossing them in the net bag Leon held open. "Whatever. They want to have us over for dinner to thank us for coaching."

"I'd love an excuse to see the wing commander's house on Andrews. Bet it's beautiful."

She groaned inwardly. Leon wasn't helping things.

"When?" he asked.

"Next weekend."

"I'm still in town. Let's do this."

His enthusiasm grated on Jackie. She felt sick thinking about seeing Colonel Dellinger at home with Veronica.

Chapter 47

The phone in her office rang, and Jackie answered it as she hit send on the email she was typing.

"Jackie, I wanted to thank you for everything you did for Sergeant Davies," Chaplain Vandesteeg said. "In addition to the OSI looking into the sexual harassment charge, the IG has been investigating Ms. Shelton and stirring up quite of bit of information on other issues. Seems like the more people they interview, the more leads they get. And it goes back years."

"About time!" Jackie felt the satisfaction of a win.

"The wing commander removed her from the group, and she is now a special assistant to the historian. He figured she can't do any damage there while they work up the paperwork to boot her."

"I hope they make it so she can't get another government job somewhere else," Jackie said.

"At the very least, she'll have a bad performance report from this job. If hiring officials take the time to look, they'll definitely steer clear of her. Oh, and the group commander has also been relieved of command. His boss felt he should have seen something wasn't right and taken action before now."

"I heard about that. So much for him retiring on time. How's Davies?" she asked.

"He stopped by just this morning. I think he's finally eating again. We discussed his next duty assignment. Getting away from this base would be good for him, so he's going to put in for an early rotation."

Jackie had an idea and opened a new email to her boss before she forgot. To Vandesteeg, she said, "I don't blame him. He didn't get much support from his peers."

"They came through eventually, but you're right. Hard to build trust with people who look the other way at the first sign of trouble."

"I agree. We need more people who do the right thing simply because it's the right thing, not because they expect something out of it." Jackie sighed.

"Colonel Cheng really set things right, and your reservists cleaned up the SARC shop in no time. The full-time replacement is due to arrive next week," Vandesteeg said.

"That's wonderful news. I have a feeling General Varn made a few calls to hurry that assignment along."

"How about you, Jackie? Anything for me to report to Carole?"

She sighed. Her only spark of interest was aimed at a married man. She didn't think that was something she wanted to share with the chaplain. "The soccer team I'm helping out with is a lot of fun."

"While I'm glad to hear that, I don't think that's what Carole is most interested in."

Jackie smiled because, although he used Carole as an excuse, she knew he was just as curious about her ability to bounce back from Stan's death. "Nothing to report at this time, but I am open to the idea when I find the right guy." *Who isn't married,* she added to herself.

They hung up, and Jackie continued typing up the email she had started. A new message popped up from Erin Mollner's lawyer. Jackie quickly clicked to open it.

"Well!" she said. "Two wins in one day."

Chapter 48

Jackie sat fuming in Congressman Olan's outer offices, waiting once again for his staffer to meet with her.

When Charlie breezed through this time, he didn't bother with an excuse for his tardiness. Jackie and Major Wilson followed him into the conference room.

Charlie didn't sit. "You have an update?"

Jackie was incredulous by the level of abruptness. "Which case?"

Two could play at this game.

He looked confused. "Kirkson."

Doesn't he realize his boss should have some interest in the McGuire case? It was in his district, after all. And he did chew me out about it in front of my boss.

"Kirkson has pled guilty. He's going into alcohol rehab as part of his plea deal. He'll serve time at Fort Leavenworth then be discharged from the Air Force under dishonorable conditions."

She waited for the expected blow back.

"I don't think Congressman Olan will need any further updates on this subject. Thank you for keeping him informed."

Charlie was out the door before she had a chance to ask any questions.

She turned on Wilson. "What was that all about?"

He covered a small laugh with his fist. "I'm not one to deal in rumors, but it seems that the congressman may have heard about Kirkson's financial troubles."

"And how would that have happened?"

Wilson's who-knows shrug was not quite innocent. "No money, no campaign donation. Seems like the congressman has more important constituents to help. They probably can't afford an expensive lawyer for their son anymore, either."

"Why didn't you tell me before we got here?"

"Your feelings about staffers aren't exactly subtle. I didn't want you to say anything you shouldn't."

Chapter 49

Jackie scrutinized the clothes in her closet, fretting over what to wear, then kicked herself because it didn't matter. *He's married! This isn't a date.*

In the end, she wore a salmon sundress with strappy sandals. There wasn't much she could do about the cast. She was tempted to leave it behind but didn't want to do anything to set back her healing. She was almost rid of the thing.

Her phone dinged with a text from Leon. Checking it, she grabbed the cookies she had baked and her purse. Locking the door behind her, Jackie texted Leon OMW while she took the stairs down to his waiting car.

"Thanks for picking me up," she said as she slid into the car. "Hi, Vicki. Are you excited to see Kendra?"

"We're going to play dolls." Vicki held up her American Girl doll for Jackie's inspection.

"Beautiful. What's your doll's name?"

"Gopher."

"Don't ask," Leon said when Jackie gave him a questioning look. He maneuvered the car into the flow of traffic heading to Andrews Air Force Base. "We got the last things for Sarah's care package. We're going to send it out tomorrow."

"These are for her." Jackie placed a bag of cookies on the console between them. "I made extra."

"She'll love them. Thanks."

They fell into a comfortable silence while Vicki sang songs to them from the backseat. Jackie stared out the window, trying to settle the butterflies in her stomach.

When they finally made it onto the base and pulled up in front of Dellinger's house, Leon said, "I thought it would be bigger."

"He's only a colonel on a base full of generals. It's still pretty big, though. Probably because he hosts official events here."

They got out of the car, and Vicki raced to ring the doorbell.

Colonel Dellinger answered the door dressed in a green polo shirt that set off his eyes. Jackie turned away so she wouldn't stare. Her throat was tight, and she desperately needed water.

"Welcome! I'm so glad you could make it." Dellinger ushered them into the house.

Vicki careened past him to find Kendra.

Jackie held out the plate of cookies. "It's not much."

Dellinger took them. "This is great, thanks. Veronica's in the kitchen. I'll let her know you're here." He gestured to the open patio door. "Make yourselves comfortable. Can I get drinks for anyone?"

They opted for white wine, and Dellinger disappeared into the kitchen. The scent of garlic and roasted peppers wafted through the kitchen door. Jackie's stomach growled. *She's probably a great cook too,* she thought.

Leon nudged Jackie with his elbow. "Told you this would be great. How often do you get a wing commander to wait on you?"

She rolled her eyes, and Leon laughed.

"What's so funny?" Dellinger came out the open door and handed them their drinks.

"Nothing, sir. We were just admiring the yard." Jackie watched the girls sitting under a tree, walking their dolls around the blanket spread on the grass.

"Please don't be so formal. You can call me David outside the office."

Jackie smiled politely but didn't see that happening. She didn't want to get any closer to this man than she already was.

"Thanks, David." Leon had no reservations about breaking this fraternization rule. Maybe it was because, as a maintainer, Leon was used to calling pilots by their callsigns, regardless of rank.

The three took seats around the table, silently sipping their wine while watching the girls play.

"Soccer has been wonderful for Kendra. She needed some way to work out her frustrations. Now when she gets in a mood, we come out here and kick the ball around." A sadness crept over Dellinger's face.

"We all need that sometimes," Leon said. "I wonder if we should set up a net in the Pentagon courtyard."

"Not a bad idea!" Dellinger raised his glass to toast Leon, though his eyes had lost their sparkle.

Jackie searched for reasons for the sorrow that had come over him.

Just then, Veronica stuck her head through the doorway. "Hello, everyone. Dinner will be ready in five minutes. Please get the girls to wash their hands." She ducked back inside.

Dellinger called the girls in.

After adding extra chairs for the two dolls who were eating with them, they settled around the table. Veronica set out the last dish heaped with broccoli and took her seat. "I hope you like chicken parmesan. It's one of Kendra's favorites."

"I love anything someone else cooks for me," Leon said. Jackie elbowed him in the side.

Colonel Dellinger extended his hands. "I hope you don't mind. We normally say grace before we start."

Tentatively, Jackie held out her hand to Leon and placed her other hand in Dellinger's. Heat rushed across her face as a spark ignited upon contact. Glancing up, she caught Dellinger's smile before he closed his eyes to pray.

Dinner was delicious, and the kids raved over Jackie's cookies. They even shared nibbles with their dolls who seemed more interested in the dessert than they had in their meals. After dinner, they ran up to Kendra's room to change the dolls' clothes.

Colonel Dellinger refilled their wine glasses and leaned back in his chair. "Veronica, this meal was wonderful, as always."

"I love the chance to cook for a larger group. You and Kendra don't eat enough."

Jackie almost flinched when Veronica patted his arm. She averted her gaze and had trouble tamping down the jealousy.

They chatted about the soccer team and the next game. "You should come help again," Leon said to Dellinger.

Under the table, Jackie kicked Leon, earning her a strange look.

"I'd love to, trust me. I just never know what my schedule will be like. Last-minute things come up, and you wouldn't be able to count on me being on time for anything."

Veronica stood and began stacking plates.

"Let me help," Jackie said.

"No, please. This is my quiet time. You sit and relax." Veronica expertly gathered the dishes and slipped into the kitchen.

"Veronica is lovely," Jackie said.

"She's great. I don't know what we'd do without her." Again, that sadness fell on him.

Even Leon must have noticed it this time because he asked, "So how did you meet?"

Dellinger swirled his glass, staring at the liquid inside. "When Kendra's mother started chemo for her cancer, she was too sick to do much around the house. We found Veronica through the au pair program."

The air disappeared from Jackie's lungs. Her heart broke hearing the melancholy in his voice. She staved off the despondence that threatened to overtake her. This wasn't about her.

He continued. "When Olive passed last year, Veronica helped me through it. She's always been there for Kendra, even when I'm working. Now she's part of the family."

Jackie's head was spinning. *So he isn't married! What does he mean by part of the family? Are they dating?*

"I'm sorry to hear about your wife," Leon said.

Mumbling something similar, Jackie was distracted replaying the interactions she had witnessed between Veronica and Dellinger, trying to put things into context with this new piece of information.

"I know what Jackie's been up to," Dellinger said to Leon. "Tell me about what you do."

Leon dove into his job description which quickly devolved into some of the funnier stories from his travels. Jackie tuned him out.

"I admit I was caught off guard when I saw you at the soccer game. I didn't know you had a daughter." Dellinger's voice was directed at Jackie, bringing her out of her musings.

"Oh, Vicki's not mine. I don't have any kids so I just kind of adopted her."

Dellinger raised his eyebrows.

Leon jumped in. "Vicki's mom is deployed right now. She should be home in a few months."

Dellinger nodded. "Well, she's lucky to have all three of you in her life then."

Glancing at his watch, Leon said, "We need to get going so Vicki doesn't miss her bedtime."

They all rose, and Dellinger called for the girls.

"Thanks again for having us over. We really appreciate it," Jackie said.

"We'll have to do it again sometime."

No way in hell, Jackie thought.

Chapter 50

"What made you suspect Preston?" Major General Varn leaned back in her desk chair and gave Jackie her full attention.

Jackie was on the edge of her seat, speaking quickly in her excitement. "At first I couldn't figure out the purpose for manufacturing these cases. Webster initially got a boost in his performance reports, which may have given him an edge for early promotion, but he didn't seem that concerned with himself. Women consistently described him as condescending and overly protective. I know I felt it. Then when he told me about his friend in college who committed suicide, that behavior fell into place for me."

She threw her hands up in frustration. "Then the Davies's thing happened, and I met a first sergeant who acted as one should. I started looking closer at Preston. I realized that Preston didn't have the same eagerness to help the troops in Webster's squadron. He was more interested in protecting Webster."

"It's sad to find a first sergeant like that. They're supposed to be the commander's connection to the enlisted troops." Varn shook her head.

"Before he was a first sergeant, he was the noncommissioned officer in charge of a flight in the same squadron as Webster. The first cases filed under Webster's name were in Preston's flight. There were others after that, but they started with Preston.

"I still couldn't figure out what benefit Preston would get out of these false reports. Then it occurred to me that Preston was feeding Webster's sick need to save women. Having found a kindred spirit in Preston, Webster kept him close."

Varn picked up a pen and clicked it a few times while she thought about what Jackie was saying.

"When Sergeant Renko and I compared Webster's assignments with Preston's, we were surprised how directly they aligned. Enlisted folks don't typically move as often as officers, so it was strange. But since Webster was a captain, Preston has followed him from one base to the next. Initially, I was so focused on Webster and his trail of sexual harassment claims, that I completely overlooked the possibility of another connection."

"What was it?"

"As Webster climbed the ladder, so did Preston. He rose in rank well ahead of his peers."

"But he had to test well to get promoted. His commander couldn't give him that," Varn pointed out.

"Agree. But the consistently high marks on his annual performance reports from Webster helped. Then I checked his medals. They were the highest allowed for his given rank at each permanent change of station with a few extra sprinkled in."

Varn nodded her understanding. "Medals are points toward promotion."

"Right. So with two out of three in the bag, Preston could concentrate on studying for his tests."

"How did you trip him up?"

"Colonel Dellinger helped me."

Varn raised an eyebrow.

Jackie blushed and chose to ignore her boss's teasing. "We asked Preston to help us find some evidence to back our concern about Webster. Conveniently, he had a file documenting discussions and misgivings he had about Webster over the same issues going back five months."

"Why would he have been documenting all that and not have brought it to anyone's attention?"

"He wasn't actually. OSI was monitoring his computer, and after Colonel Dellinger planted the idea in his head, Preston went back to his office and created the whole thing from scratch."

"But it's pretty easy to see when an electronic file has been created. He couldn't fake that unless he really knows computers."

"He didn't. He just opened a file that was created five months ago and overwrote the data with what he wanted us to see. Before he sent the file to Colonel Dellinger, he made an entry about our meeting, which set the date modified to the current date."

"What's going to happen now?"

"Preston will, at the very least, get an article fifteen. He was the one who made up many of the stories to start the unrestricted reports. Colonel Dellinger is having the OSI do a thorough investigation on him to see if we missed anything."

"Was he the one who attacked you?"

Jackie shook her head. "OSI checked his car and found a few scratches. There was paint from the car that hit me on what was left of my bike. They are going to compare and see if it matches up. But Preston has a solid alibi for the night I was attacked in Shirlington."

"What's going to happen to Colonel Webster?"

"Webster is still being relieved of command for lack of confidence. Colonel Dellinger feels he should have noticed the pattern himself and investigated it more closely. In Webster's attempt to help those women, he hurt others. Colonel Dellinger is reexamining all the cases Webster reported at Andrews. He's working with Air Force Inspector General to look into the past cases."

"We'll have to brief the secretary. Pull your bullet points together. I'll give Colonel Dellinger a heads up."

Jackie sensed the end of their conversation and stood. "Yes, ma'am."

"I have to take back what I said about you not being an investigator. Maybe you got into the wrong line of work."

Chapter 51

Sitting in her cubicle on the fourth floor, Jackie tuned into C-SPAN to watch the secretary of the Air Force answer questions from the press on the first floor of the Pentagon. As soon as they had briefed him, he had his staff set up the press conference so they could get ahead of the news and make sure it was spun the way he wanted it to spin. Major General Varn, in her full-dress uniform, stood to the side and slightly behind the secretary, ready to support him if necessary.

The news of the reinvestigation of over a dozen sexual assault and harassment cases was going to bring a lot of unwanted attention from both sides of the argument. Some felt the military wasn't doing enough to stop these attacks. Others argued that men were the victims, having to watch their step around women who could cry wolf at any time.

Jackie didn't envy her boss or the secretary. There wasn't much more they could be doing. She wondered how Colonel Dellinger was fairing. The attention on his wing couldn't be good for his career, either.

When the press conference was over, Jackie turned her attention to the resume she had requested from Sergeant Davies. He had good performance reports and tested well for promotion. If the interview went well with Major General Varn,

Jackie was sure he would be a good addition to the SAPRO team. They needed a man to provide a different perspective on cases and develop the new curriculum to underscore that men could also be sexually harassed. She could think of no better candidate.

Chapter 52

The season was almost over. The kids and their parents were celebrating with a picnic, complete with water balloons and ice cream. Leon was manning the grill when Jackie delivered a large thermos of iced tea.

"This was a great idea," he told her, dishing out another hamburger to a waiting parent.

"I'm not going to take the credit. Some of the parents corralled me into it. I just reserved the spot."

Colonel Dellinger approached the grill, plate at the ready. "I see you are more than a coach," he said to Leon.

"Wait until you taste my burgers before you make that decision." He flipped a burger onto Dellinger's plate.

"No more cast. That's a good sign."

It took Jackie a second to realize Dellinger was speaking to her. Her mind had been searching for an excuse to be anywhere else. "Uh, yes. I'm still supposed to be careful with it, but the bones are back where they should be."

"Where's Veronica?" Leon asked.

"Sundays are her day off, and she had a date." The smile was proud, as if this were a personal accomplishment. "She works too hard. I've been trying to get her involved in activities outside of Kendra's circles so she could meet people her age. Seems like the board game group at the local library did the trick."

Jackie's heart thundered. *Did I hear correctly? He's not with Veronica?*

Leon's phone buzzed. "Jackie, take over, will you?"

She took the spatula as he hurried away.

"Is everything okay? He looked worried," Dellinger said.

"He's been waiting on a call from Sarah. They keep changing the return date for her TDY."

"Sarah is Vicki's mother, right?"

"Yep. They've been married about ten years, but this is the longest they've been apart since Vicki was born." Jackie continued flipping the burgers. She glanced up and caught Dellinger staring at her. The heat rushed to her face, and she hoped she could blame it on the grill.

"I thought . . ." he trailed off.

She broke eye contact long enough to deliver hot dogs to the waiting children.

When she turned back to him, he was shaking his head slowly, laughing to himself.

"What's so funny?" Jackie asked.

"Nothing. Nothing at all."

"Daddy!" Kendra called. "Will you push me on the swing?" She ran up and took hold of his free hand, dragging him toward the playground.

He gave Jackie a helpless look and let himself be propelled away.

She stared after him, a thousand things running through her mind. Every interaction they had together must be reevaluated and cataloged. She needed to talk to her sister.

Chapter 53

OSI checked the scratches on Preston's car to see if it was a match with the car that hit me. No go. Besides, he parks in a garage with surveillance, and his car didn't leave the lot that night." Jackie grabbed a fry off Leon's plate.

They sat in the Pentagon food court, after finishing strategizing the last soccer game to make sure everyone had equal playing time. Now they were avoiding going back to work.

"Who else could it have been?" Leon asked.

"I'm not sure. Maybe it was just an accident. I wouldn't be the first hit and run in DC."

"No way. You said a car followed you from the bus stop, then you got hit. Then someone attacked you on your way back to your apartment. Oh, and let's not forget your apartment was broken into. That's too much to be a coincidence. Even you aren't that unlucky."

"Well, the Davies's case is settled. Shelton got her walking papers, and she supposedly has friends in all kinds of places."

"Did you mention that to the cops?" He finished his fries and collected the trash from the table.

"It's hearsay. Besides, she's out of their jurisdiction. They don't have anything to go on."

"What about that case at Wright-Pat?"

"Kirkson? He's already been moved to Leavenworth to serve his sentence. Besides the victim, I don't think anyone but the congressman and his staffer know of my involvement. They aren't going to get anything out of harming me."

Leon crossed his arms and leaned both elbows on the table. "Could Webster have been messing with you?"

"Not really his style. His god complex has him saving women, not harming them."

He stood and grabbed the food tray. "I don't like this. Something isn't right."

Chapter 54

The park was eerily quiet after the usual squeals and laughter from the dozen kids. The last game had finished, and Dellinger had stayed to help Jackie and Leon clean up. Kendra went home with Veronica, but not until she hugged Jackie's legs.

When Leon's truck was loaded and Vicki was buckled in, he made an excuse about having to get going right away. "Sorry, Jackie. I can't give you a ride home. Vicki and I have a few stops to make. David, would you mind?"

Jackie wanted to crawl under a rock. "I can find my own way home."

At the same time, Dellinger said, "Of course. No problem."

Leon didn't wait around for the awkwardness to dissipate. He jumped in his truck and took off.

Jackie stared after him, not wanting to look at Colonel Dellinger.

"Sir, you don't—"

"I would really prefer it if you called me David."

She met his eyes then. "Okay, David. I catch the bus here all the time. I can get home myself."

"I was hoping for a chance to talk to you outside of work anyway." He looked almost bashful, and Jackie's breath caught.

"Do you want to walk a bit?" he asked.

"Sure."

They walked slowly toward the trail around the park. The trees cast long shadows as the sun was tucking itself in for the night. The cicadas sang their courting song.

Although the evening was awash in the noise of nature, the silence between Jackie and Dellinger grew until she thought she would explode.

With a rush of air, Dellinger let out a long sigh. "I thought you and Leon were a couple."

Jackie laughed. It was the last thing she had expected him to say. "No way. He and Sarah took me in when I first moved to DC. He's been trying to fix me up on dates for years." She realized what she said and shut her mouth quickly.

Dellinger ran a hand over his face, cupping his chin in a thoughtful gesture. "That makes so much more sense now. Leon's been trying to get me to help with the team, but I couldn't bring myself to—"

"What?"

He stopped walking, and Jackie turned to face him.

"You impress me, Jackie. You have since the first day I met you."

Her heart raced. She couldn't believe her ears. "I thought you were with Veronica." Her voice was almost a whisper.

It was his turn to laugh. "She is way too young for me and not at all my type."

Jackie was trying to get up the courage to ask what his type was when Dellinger's eyes went wide, and he pushed her aside.

The sizzling in the air was followed by Dellinger's form hitting the hard ground. The resounding crack of his head hitting a rock lining the path sent the nearby birds into flight.

Jackie cried out and dropped to her knees at his side. She followed the wires back to the taser held in the hands of Technical Sergeant Buckley.

"What the hell!" Jackie yelled. She ripped the electrodes from his bare arms.

"You ruined my life," Buckley roared.

"What are you talking about?" Jackie searched Dellinger's head, finding blood seeping from his scalp. His eyes were closed, and he wasn't reacting to the yelling going on around him.

"Do you have any idea what I went through after that scumbag raped me? Now I have to relive it, just because you couldn't let it go." Buckley pulled a gun from under her long jacket and waved it in Jackie's direction.

Jackie stripped off her sweatshirt and pressed it to Dellinger's wound, trying to ignore the fear rising in her chest. "What's going on has nothing to do with your case."

"Colonel Webster saved my life. I'm not going to let you discredit him with your witch hunt!"

"Webster has hurt so many people. Whether he meant to or not, things must be set right." Jackie stood now and placed herself between Dellinger and Buckley.

"Colonel Webster saved me," she repeated. "This is still a man's Air Force. They take and they take. If we aren't willing to give, they take what they want anyway. You should know! Women have to work twice as hard for everything. Then it can be shattered simply because they're bigger than we are."

Buckley was shaking, tears streaming down her face. "The Air Force is reexamining my case. That bastard may get out of jail. All because you had to poke your nose in where it doesn't belong."

"I'm doing my job." Jackie labored to keep her voice calm.

"Colonel Webster helped so many people." Buckley swiped at her tears.

"What about the innocent people whose lives he wrecked? They were victims too." Jackie tried not to look into the barrel pointed at her. "We aren't releasing the bad guys. We're just saving the ones who deserve to be saved."

"You don't know that!" The gun shook as Buckley jabbed at Jackie with her words. "What if he goes free?"

Jackie raised her hands, palm out. "You have to trust the system. They aren't going to release the guilty. The problem is, we may have been too hard on the innocent in our zeal to get the bad guys. We've forced some good airmen out of the service based on accusations that weren't substantiated. Or destroyed their careers over hearsay. Is that fair?"

On the ground, Dellinger moaned and turned his head. As Buckley swung the gun toward him, Jackie moved to block her aim. A figure from the trees hurled into Buckley, tackling her to the ground. The gun skittered away.

Buckley screamed curses as Webster flipped her face down, pulling her arms behind her back. In no time, he secured the cuffs on her wrists. Talking over her rants, he got her attention. She calmed down enough to listen to him. He moved her into a sitting position and wrapped his arms around her shoulders, all the while whispering soothing words into her ear.

Jackie rushed to Dellinger's side, helping him as he tried to sit up. He winced when his hand found the bloody spot on his head.

Sirens got closer as a squad car bounded over the grassy park, the ambulance not far behind.

Dellinger lifted his hand to shield his eyes from the headlights piercing through his injured head.

The police officers jumped from their car, weapons raised, taking in the scene.

Webster called out. "I'm Lieutenant Colonel Robert Webster, commander of the security force squadron at Andrews Air Force Base. I'm the one who called. I'm unarmed but there's a gun on the ground about twenty feet to my right."

One of the cops hustled over and kicked the gun further away.

"Lillian, I'm going to let you go now," Webster said calmly. "But I will be here for you. Do you understand?"

The woman shook her head from side to side. "Don't let me go!"

"It's all right. Let's see if we can get up together."

The cops lowered their weapons but didn't holster them as Webster guided Buckley to her feet.

He held her close, and she sobbed into his chest. Calmly, he said, "Officers, do you think you could give us a ride to base?"

Epilogue

Jackie turned up the volume on her television when Congressman Olan stepped to the bank of microphones outside the Capitol Building.

"It's appalling what our servicemembers put up with. Sexual harassment is never acceptable in any situation. That's why my office stays on top of these cases to ensure the military commanders do their jobs."

Jackie almost gagged at his righteous indignation. He went on. "Many people have the misconception that a woman cannot be the aggressor in these cases. Well, it's sad to say that we have proven once again that women are as capable as men in another way."

Laughter burst from Jackie's lips. How was he going to dig himself out of that stupid statement?

A staffer came to his side and whispered in his ear.

"That's all I have to say at this time. I have other work to attend to." The congressman gave a feeble wave as his staffer led him away from the barrage of cameras and to a waiting vehicle.

She muted the TV and went back to her dinner.

Her phone dinged. She read the text message from Colonel Dellinger. "You watching the news?"

"Yes."

"Want to discuss?"

Before she could respond, another came in. "Over dinner?"

Jackie's heart flipped. *Was this a casual ask or a date?*

Her thumbs hovered over the keypad. Before she could chicken out, she typed, "Where?"

236

#####

Like *Truth Has No Agenda*?

Learn more about Jackie in *The Obsession* and *Wind the Clock.*

As always, we would appreciate a review on any media that is easiest for you.

About the Author

Colonel (retired) DAWN BROTHERTON is an award-winning author and featured speaker. When it comes to exceptional writing, Dawn draws on her experience as a retired colonel from the U.S. Air Force as well as a softball coach, Girl Scout leader, and quilter. Her books include the Jackie Austin Mysteries, cozy mystery *Eastover Treasures*, YA Fantasy *The Dragons of Silent Mountain*, and romance *Untimely Love*.

She has also completed four books (*Trish's Team; Margie Makes a Difference; Nicole's New Friend,* and *Tammy Tries Baseball*) in the middle grade Lady Tigers series, encouraging female athletes to reach for the stars in the game they love.

With the help of former Disney illustrator Chad Thompson, Dawn has released her first children's picture book (ages 3-7) *If I Look Like You* and its accompanying activity book, *Scout and Her Friends*. These books help children explore STEM and non-STEM career fields as they learn they do not have to change who they are to fit in.

Under nonfiction, the *Baseball/Softball Scorebook* was created with instructions written for those not as familiar with the intricacies of the game.

The Road to Publishing is designed to walk writers through the maze of becoming a published author, whether self-publishing, traditional-publishing, or somewhere in between.

Dawn is a contributing author to the non-fiction *A-10s over Kosovo,* sharing stories from her deployment, and *Water from Wellspring,* a collection of short stories about how God has worked in people's lives.

Her most recent project is *Sisters in Arms: Inspiring Generations.* This book is written by women military veterans passing on their life lessons to the generations who come after them.

For more information about Dawn's books and book signings, go to www.DawnBrothertonAuthor.com.

Keep in touch with Dawn via the web:

Website: https://www.dawnbrothertonauthor.com/
Facebook: https://www.facebook.com/DawnBrothertonAuthor
Instagram: https://www.instagram.com/dawnbrothertonauthor/
Bookbub: https://www.bookbub.com/authors/dawn-brotherton
Goodreads: https://www.goodreads.com/author/show/7867237.Dawn_Brotherton